Karl suppressed a shudder as he looked at the instrument panel.

The ship was jockeying into position to leave its temporary orbit around Mars. As it entered the atmosphere, its speed would increase 1,200 miles per hour and the pilot would need to fire the brake thrusters to slow it down. Then, in precisely the right sequence, he would need to release the huge nose-cone parachute. Karl knew that from that second on, he would have no control until the land thrusters were needed.

He nearly jumped when someone tapped his shoulder from behind. Ian McShane handed him a towel.

"I figured you'd need this just about now," the Irish boy said, grinning. "My hands are sweating too."

"Thank you," Karl said, wiping his hands quickly, not taking his eyes off the monitor.

Ian clapped him on the back. "Okay now, boyo! Bring it in nice and easy. You've got all the time in the—"

Suddenly, the computer navcon screen flashed its orders:

INITIATE ENTRY SEQUENCE—NOW!

It was time. . . .

JACK ANDERSON PRESENTS ...

The YOUNG ASTRONAUTS

#4 DESTINATION MARS
RICK NORTH

ZEBRA BOOKS
KENSINGTON PUBLISHING CORP.

ZEBRA BOOKS

are published by

Kensington Publishing Corp.
475 Park Avenue South
New York, NY 10016

First printing: January, 1991

Printed in the United States of America

To Rick Sternbach and
G. Harry Stine

Chapter One

Through the radio link inside their helmets, the one hundred thirty-five crew members of the Mars ship *Santa Maria*, strapped into their safety harnesses in the long corridors, could hear the voices from the bridge.

"Manual control linkage?" That was Dr. Mary Elizabeth Allen's crisp voice. Dr. Allen was the Mars expedition's chief medical officer, and the *Santa Maria*'s first-shift pilot.

"Check. MCL online." And that was Karl, Nathan Long realized with a little jolt of excitement. One of his own team had been chosen to be first-shift copilot.

"Force stability augmenters?"

"Check. Online."

"Atmospheric pressure control?"

"Affirmative on O_2 inflow." Karl's voice seemed to waver with uncertainty for a moment. "Still getting a

7

red light on nitrogen inflow balance."

"Confirmed." Dr. Allen would be getting the same reading on her own control panel. "Stand by, copilot. Mission Control, this is the *Santa Maria*. We have a red light on nitrogen inflow pressure. Do you copy?"

What that meant, Nathan knew, was that the atmosphere inside the huge ship had not yet been balanced to the exact nitrogen/oxygen percentages found on Earth, the kind of air they were used to breathing. That was only one reason that everyone on board was in full flight suit, complete with sealed helmet and independent oxygen supply.

We really do look like men from Mars, Nathan thought, twisting as far as he could in his restraint harness to see several dozen similar figures up and down the corridors.

There were small video screens set at intervals in the corridor. Nathan could just see one through the extreme right-hand side of his helmet visor. It showed a rear-angle view of a tranquil, cloudy blue Earth from one of the *Santa Maria*'s E.V.A. cameras, filming through the support struts of the Icarus orbiting space platform that had been the pioneers' home these past several months.

Good-bye, Earth! Nathan thought, trying not to say it aloud. Not that anyone could hear it unless he had his outgoing channel open, but he didn't want anyone thinking he was some sentimental crybaby. Good-bye, Earth! Good-bye, Mom! Don't worry; I'll be fine.

Nathan caught Lisette's eye across the corridor.

8

The dark-eyed French-Canadian girl's enthusiasm was so strong he could feel it from where he stood. If it weren't for her, Nathan thought, I might chicken out even now.

Not everyone in the ship's corridors could see the vid screens, so listening to the radio voices from the flying bridge and from Mission Control back on Icarus was very important to know what was going on. If you could hear past the pounding of your own heart.

There was also a lot of local chatter, and if you kept your incoming channel open, you could eavesdrop on your neighbors.

". . . You should have thought of that before you suited up!" Alice scolded Noemi, who, strapped in beside her, had already found something to complain about. "You'll be all right once we make it through the departure sequence."

"And you'll be contributing to the recycled water supply," Genshiro offered cheerfully from the other side of the corridor.

"Gen, please!" Alice said. Everyone knew the ship's water supply came partly from closed-system recycling of waste water, but nobody wanted to think about the mechanics of it too much.

"The important thing, Noemi," Gen went on mischievously, as if Alice hadn't spoken, "is not to think about running water. You know, flowing rivers, waterfalls, pounding surf—"

"Gen!" Noemi protested.

"Yes, Gen, please stop!" Sergei added from farther

down the corridor, next to Nathan. Gen gave him a puzzled look through his visor. "Well, I have sometimes had the same difficulty myself."

" 'Sometimes'?" Gen asked innocently.

"All right, now!" Sergei admitted. "We all have too much adrenaline in our systems or something. We can't all be as cool as you. No more talk about running water."

"Oh, brother!" Lanie sighed, restless already. "If you guys don't shut up!"

"It's no big deal," Tara White, the tall black girl from New York City said. "During the very first American Mercury mission, Astronaut Alan Shepard had to—"

"Tara—" Lanie pleaded.

"Just trying to help," she said, a little upset at Lanie's attitude.

Uh-oh, Lanie thought. Trouble. Me and my big mouth!

"Affirmative on nitrogen input now, Dr. Allen." Karl's voice broke through the local chatter and everyone quieted down and listened.

"Confirmed," Dr. Allen said. "Looks like we're finally cooking. *Santa Maria* to Mission Control. We have a green on all systems. Repeat: we have a green for go on all systems."

"Roger, *Santa Maria* . . ." the Mission Control operator's voice crackled from Icarus. "*Nina* and *Pinta* also show green. Stand by for departure sequence, *Santa Maria* . . ."

They could hear the thrusters firing in test sequence: synchronized bursts to port, then to starboard, then shutdown. The ship was still attached to the supply umbilicals and restraint tethers, so it wasn't going anywhere yet. But the thrusters on either side of the huge cigar-shaped vessel would run the test sequence until Dr. Allen got the go-ahead from Mission Control.

Once the umbilicals and restraints were detached, inertia and the thruster bursts would slide the ship slowly out of its dock. Then the thrusters had to be fired manually to turn the ship toward the proper trajectory to reach Mars. Course corrections would continue throughout the two-hundred-twenty-day day journey. As huge as they were, the three ships would behave no differently in zero G than a human body would. The principles of motion were the same.

Mission Control would decide the order in which the ships would depart. Nathan not so secretly hoped the *Santa Maria* would be first. It was unofficially designated the expedition's flagship, but that didn't necessarily mean anything. The decision might have something to do with the way the ships were berthed. The *Santa Maria* was in the middle. The *Nina* was to her left, the *Pinta* to her right. Port and starboard, Nathan reminded himself. The *Nina*'s at portside, *Pinta*'s at starboard.

Port and starboard for left and right, fore and aft for front and back. Before the To Mars Together program, these had been words from old pirate movies, secret codes Nathan had never bothered checking out. Now the nautical terminology, used in the space program from the beginning, was as much second nature as telling time or knowing the multiplication table.

The thrusters test-fired again. In between, everyone on board could still hear the conversation from the flying bridge.

"Weapons check?" Dr. Allen asked Karl without taking her eyes off her own control panel.

She trusted the German kid. He was good, the best of the copilot trainees, but Dr. Allen wasn't going to let it go to his head. She was going to drive him just as hard as, maybe harder than, anyone else under her command.

"Weapons check, affirmative," the blond boy replied. His English was flawless, with only the slightest hint of an accent. According to his personnel file, he was fluent in several other languages as well. Dr. Allen watched him swallow nervously.

"Problem, copilot?"

"It's this idea of weapons," Karl blurted out. "I know the Blaster is intended only for breaking up asteroids, but—"

"*B*road-*R*ange *L*aser *Aster*oid Armament." Dr. Allen gave it its official name. "Designed for breaking up any stray hunks of rock diverted from the asteroid belt between Mars and Jupiter and floating in interplanetary space. If you were in the jungle, you'd want a knife to cut through the vines in your path, wouldn't you? Same principle. Once we reach Mars, the Blaster will be dismantled and used for peaceful purposes, as will everything else on board."

The ships had been constructed in space from modular units shuttled up from Earth. Everyone aboard had helped to put them together, starting with the strange structural skeletons, and ending up with something halfway between a huge cigar and the Goodyear blimp. Even with the solar-panel wings extended to catch the sun's rays for energy, they weren't graceful; they were downright ugly. Gen and Lanie had secretly christened them "Pigs in Space."

But they were practical. Instead of being left wastefully in orbit, or decaying uselessly on the surface as the Viking landers had been, these ships would be used. Every piece of equipment, from the computers to the seat cushions, would be taken apart and used in the construction of the Mars colony.

"I know that, Dr. Allen," Karl said, a little defensively. He had great respect for the expedition's chief medical officer. She was not only a physician but a NASA-trained shuttle pilot, good enough to head the "flying crew" on the way to Mars. "It's just that the very idea of a weapon of any kind — well, a weapon is a weapon. Even if it's designed for peaceful uses, it could be used for harm."

"So can a plastic fork, if you know how to use it," Dr. Allen reminded him. "And this particular plastic fork may in the not so distant future save our lives."

Nathan wished everyone would just shut up and

enjoy the view. Didn't they realize that within a few days the only world mankind had ever lived on would be reduced to just another anonymous speck of light in the night sky?

He supposed as team leader he could tell his own people to keep it down just a little, but Sergei was still hyper about what had happened with Lisette, and Nathan didn't know if it was safe to talk to him without getting his head bitten off. And he was in charge of his team only when they were working *as* a team. Here on the ships, the rules were different.

And if the chatter was really getting to him, all he had to do was shut off his headset. But that would leave him totally isolated in the little world inside his suit. Nathan needed other people, even if they sometimes drove him crazy.

"I know!" he heard Alice say. Nathan snapped back to reality. Was she talking to him? Her blue eyes met his brown eyes through their helmet visors.

The thrusters continued to fire in sequence. The voices from the bridge continued their reassuring systems-check. And the local chatter went on.

"Warp speed, Mr. Scott!" Gen wisecracked as the thruster sequence increased. Gen knew that meant the last of the umbilicals connecting the *Santa Maria* to Icarus had dropped away. Within minutes Mission Control would announce the departure order, the restraint tethers would fall away, and—

"Warp speed?" Alice echoed him. "What's that all about?"

"Never mind!" the Japanese boy said, thinking:

14

Don't tell me they don't show *Trek* reruns in New Zealand! Alice was still waiting for him to explain. "Oh, all right! It's a saying from an ancient samurai tale—"

"We've just been given our flight order, people," Dr. Allen announced. "We're going to be third. First the *Nina*, then the *Pinta*, then us."

Everybody groaned. Dr. Allen could hear it through her headset.

"It isn't going to make any difference in the long run. We'll be exchanging places a great deal over the next several months. Besides, this is a cooperative effort, not a horse race. Let's try to keep that in mind."

Every one of the trainees was crazy about Dr. Allen. Of the three adults aboard the *Santa Maria*, she was probably everyone's favorite.

Not that there was anything to dislike about Dr. Al-Wahab or Dr. Berger, but both men were usually so preoccupied with their work that it was hard to get their attention.

Dr. Ali Al-Wahab was the *Santa Maria*'s engineer. Everything from the computers to the electrical system to the thruster engines to the waste-disposal system was his responsibility. If he seemed preoccupied, it was because he knew that every life on board depended on his ability to keep everything up and running.

Dr. Ari Berger was the expedition's chief agronomist, in charge of the hydroponic labs aboard all three ships. This meant that not only did the expedition's present and future food supply depend on him,

15

but the constant recycling of carbon dioxide into breathable oxygen relied upon what Dr. Berger called his "little green men."

Dr. Berger would be the first to admit he had a weird sense of humor. Ever since Jules Verne's early science fiction stories in the nineteenth century, people had made jokes about "little green men" on Mars. Dr. Berger claimed it was the other way around. It was the Earth ships which would be bringing the little green men *to* Mars, in the form of hundreds of thousands of fruit and vegetable seedlings.

Both men were also trained pilots, as capable as Dr. Allen was of piloting the ship, and each would rotate shifts with her so that someone had hands-on control at all times. With their state-of-the-art computer interface, and radio remote from Mission Control at least until the midpoint of their journey, the three ships could practically fly themselves. But the human touch was necessary to get each ship out of spacedock and on the correct trajectory. The human touch was necessary for troubleshooting along the way, and for hands-on control during soft landing.

And all of it was about to happen any minute now.

"Hey, guys, look!" Nathan shouted suddenly. For all the noise and chaos around him, he'd never really taken his eyes off the E.V.A. screen. "It's the *Nina*. She's moving out!"

Necks craned, bodies shifted against their restraint tethers. Space suits creaked, and more than once two people knocked helmets in their eagerness to get a

16

look.

"Wow!"

"Yes!"

"Fantastic!"

"Oh, cool!"

"Way to go! Awwright!"

The cheers and comments filled the airwaves.

The reaction was the same a few minutes later as the *Pinta* also slid out of her berth, and Dr. Allen rotated the *Santa Maria*'s E.V.A. camera in her direction. The cheering had begun to die down when Dr. Allen's voice came through again.

"Okay, people, listen up. We are on a sixty-second countdown—mark. I don't need to remind you that we'll be experiencing a point-five-G force as we accelerate. If we were under normal Earth conditions, you wouldn't feel a thing, but after all this time in zero G, some of you may experience a slight dizziness or nausea. Remember your breathing exercises to control the nausea. Thirty seconds—mark."

It wasn't necessary for Dr. Allen to give them the countdown. All they had to do was watch the digital display on the video screens. Or listen to their own heartbeats.

For a second or two it was absolutely, deathly quiet. Then Nathan was aware of murmurs, whispers, prayers.

"Three . . . two . . . one . . ." he found himself saying in spite of himself.

There was no actual "blastoff," nothing like the way it felt in a shuttle pulling out of Earth gravity at up to three G. It was more like a gigantic hand pushing on your stomach, trying to squeeze all the air out of you. Nathan could hear everyone around him breathing harder.

"Bozhe moi!" Sergei said in Russian.

"Madre de Dios . . ." Noemi prayed. If you listened hard you could probably hear all of the major languages of Earth as the *Santa Maria* began to move.

Watching the E.V.A. screen, you'd swear it was Icarus that was slipping backward while the *Santa Maria* stayed in one place. There was no feeling of movement from the ship itself, only that huge hand on your stomach—which didn't seem to be pressing so hard now—and the sound of the ship's thrusters on a single, long burn.

The burn lasted about five minutes by the digital readout, and was replaced by a series of sporadic bursts. Dr. Allen was adjusting the trajectory manually. When the *Santa Maria's* actual trajectory lined up exactly with the computer's projection, the intermittent bursts would stop, the thrusters would shut down, and the ship would begin its "free fall" toward Mars.

Everyone on board had had a turn on the bridge simulator when the instructors were choosing the best candidates for the copilots' course. Each of them could close their eyes now and see the trajectory readout in their minds. Only Karl had the real thing in front of him. His knuckles were white as he held the controls.

"How's it going?" Dr. Allen asked him.

"It is not as easy as driving a Mercedes down the autobahn," Karl admitted. "But it's wonderful!"

One final long burn nudged the *Santa Maria* on course, then everything went silent.

Gen was the first to break the silence. "Is that it?"

Chapter Two

"Yeah, that's it," Nathan said, releasing the restraint tether with one hand and the pressure seal on his helmet with the other. They'd practiced this part for weeks. "Time to move out."

Nathan was the first to remove his helmet and sniff the air in the spacecraft. Not exactly a spring breeze, he decided. Not a summer night after a big thunderstorm, either. And nothing like the lobby of a tenplex theater with the popcorn machine going, but it was breathable, about as neutral as the filtered air on Icarus. After a while, Nathan thought, I'll even forget what Earth smells like.

He reached across the corridor and squeezed Lisette's hand.

"Best of luck!" she said cheerily before they split up, knowing Sergei would be watching them. Around them, everyone else was popping their helmets and breathing deeply.

"Ice hockey rink!" Sergei announced.

"Jumbo jet," someone contradicted him.

"Shopping mall!" Lanie overrode them both. "Minus the pizza. Bummer, I'm homesick already!"

She slipped out of her restraint tether, locked her helmet onto a Velcro waist-loop, and started grabbing for the handhold rails at waist level throughout the corridors. These alternated with Velcro patches on the "floors" and "ceilings," which meshed with the Velcro heels of their socks. The teams grouped together to head for the rec room and collect their gear.

"What you can't stow in a standard locker, you can't bring aboard," Dr. Thompson and the other instructors had drilled into them over and over while they were in training. Dr. Thompson had been assigned to the *Nina*. Over the next few months he would be as much as a hundred thousand miles away from them, but his voice still echoed in their heads. "What you can't bring aboard, you can't bring along."

Dr. Al-Wahab, rubbing his thick mustache, his eyes shy behind their thick glasses, had put it differently: "The most important thing in space *is* space," he had said in his soft voice.

"Too Zen!" Gen had commented at the time, getting a laugh, but everyone knew what Dr. Al-Wahab meant.

The ships were designed to maximize space, but every centimeter of that space had to be utilized. Food and partial water supplies, not only for the journey but as backup for their first year on Mars, fuel for the thrusters, every tool and item of equipment they would need to construct a space colony, clothing, medical supplies—everything had to be brought along. Robot ships had been sent ahead to

21

transport some supplies and heavy equipment, but most of what the pioneers needed they would be bringing with them.

There simply wasn't room for everything everyone wanted to bring.

All of them had spent hours of rec time exploring different and ingenious ways to stuff "personals" into a space the size of the locker each of them would be assigned in their four- or five-person roomettes aboard the ships. Empty, the lockers seemed roomy enough; once the packing began, the available space would disappear incredibly fast.

"Homesick? What have you got to be homesick about?" Gen teased Lanie as they scrambled over other moving bodies to find their duffels in the nets hanging from the rec room bulkheads. "I thought you couldn't wait to get out here?"

"I couldn't — can't," Lanie said. "That doesn't mean I can't miss pizza."

Figure Lanie to miss something so ordinary, Nathan thought, finding his duffel more by the familiar shape of his skateboard than by the standard name tag. He was more bummed by the fact that the E.V.A. screen had gone to static as soon as the thrusters began the long burn. Probably the cameras had had to be pulled into their housings at the last minute, and he hadn't gotten a last look at Earth.

It was out there, all right, right behind them, big and blue and bursting with life. It had dominated their sky the whole time they were on Icarus, but Nathan couldn't seem to get enough. He'd wanted to watch it shrink in size against the background of space; now it was too late. The flying bridge was pointed away from Earth; the pilot and copilot would be concentrating on the space before them. The E.V.A. cameras would be used only for maintenance from now on, scanning the ship's hull on the lookout for damage or possibly dangerous situations. If they caught a glimpse of Earth, it would be purely by accident.

Nathan hugged the board to his chest so hard it hurt. He'd had all that time on Icarus to say his farewells to Earth. Why was he so bummed out now?

And why had he brought his dumb board along anyway? He sure couldn't use it on the *Santa Maria*, and he'd be much too busy to use it once they got to Mars. It was taking up valuable space he could have used for something else.

Like what? Nathan asked himself. Nothing else he owned was as valuable to him as his board. Suddenly a big grin spread over his face. He was thinking of the kind of turns he could do at .38 G, Mars normal.

Sleeping quarters aboard the Mars ships consisted of small roomettes, like zero-G college dorm rooms. Most of them were eight-sided, and four people could fit fairly comfortably. Only the ones at the corners of the corridors had an extra space for a fifth person. It had something to do with the basic interior design of each ship, as Gen had explained to anyone who wanted to listen.

"Eight sides is more efficient," the Japanese rocker had explained. "If you look at the blueprint schematic, you'll see that the units are stacked at forty-five-degree angles, like the inside of a beehive. It saves space, until you get to the corners."

Each of the adults earned a private, one-person room, and these fitted into the overall design by leaving one five-sided shape at each corner.

Lanie and Alice and Noemi and Lisette had gotten along so well this far that they'd hoped they wouldn't be split up or assigned a fifth roommate.

"You guessed it!" Lanie complained, slinging her duffel into one corner of the five-person roomette. It swung back at her and she grabbed it. "As if life wasn't complicated enough!"

Each roomette had its own high-pressure shower/toilet facility, similar to the ones on Icarus. Each of the five corners contained a zippered sleep-sack with a restraint tether. Beside each sleep-sack was a reading lamp, Velcro panels for hanging up personal possessions, and a locker with a combination lock built into each bulkhead. There was only one PC per roomette.

Dressing, sleeping, reading, studying—all had to be dealt with in this small space. Five or even four people couldn't all fit into a roomette and remove their red jump suits simultaneously, as most of the teams were beginning to find out now that everyone had retrieved their belongings from the rec room.

Fortunately, each set of roommates would be divided into two shifts, so that at least two people would be somewhere else on the ship—working, studying, exercising, eating, hanging out—while the rest were sleeping. But there was no such thing as complete privacy, no chance to be alone.

"We were so tight. Who needs a fifth wheel?" Lanie lamented. When she saw the name tag on the locker next to hers, she groaned out loud. "Oh, no!"

Not Tara White. Not after the attitude they'd been giving each other during launch.

"The feeling's mutual!" Tara slipped between Alice and Lisette and swung her locker open, practically knocking Lanie aside. She stuffed her entire duffel into the locker unopened, then shut it and spun the combination lock. "Not to worry, Lanie Rizzo. You and I are on opposite shifts. If we're lucky, we won't even have to look at each other for this entire trip!"

With that she pushed out of the roomette without a word to the other three. Lanie, just floated in mid-air with her mouth open. What was going on here?

Tara seemed to think she was a snob or something. Well, she wasn't. She hated snobs and phonies, but otherwise she went out of her way to get along with everyone. But it was the New York girl's whole attitude that got to her—the way she slammed in and out, the defiant way she spun the combination lock on her locker. No one expected anyone to steal anything, but the locks were there as a kind of mental backup; everyone understood that. The thing was to lock your locker without making it some kind of obnoxious move, making it look as if you didn't trust

25

your roomies. Lanie noticed Alice and Lisette and Noemi watching her.

"What'd I say?" she demanded. "Did you hear me say anything? I'm just standing here, and she comes on with this attitude! Why is it my fault?"

"You must have said something." Noemi shrugged, studying her perfect face and as much of her perfect figure as she could see in the tiny mirror built into each locker door.

Dress regulations gave the pioneers a choice between wearing the red coverall or a T-shirt-and-shorts combination. Noemi preferred the T-shirt-and-shorts combo; it showed off her legs. Her long black hair — too long for zero G, everyone kept telling her — floated luxuriously around her face, making her look like a mermaid. Of course, it also got into her eyes and her mouth, and sometimes even into the equipment, but that didn't seem to bother Noemi. Now she fixed her dark eyes on Lanie, accusing.

"You two had better learn to get along, since we all have to be squashed in together like this!"

Lisette just smiled and shrugged.

"Keep me out of this!" she said, and was soon on her way out of the room.

Alice, methodically stowing T-shirts and shorts on the same shelf in her locker so they would be handy when she needed them, didn't say anything at first.

"Well?" Lanie demanded. She wanted this thing settled. "What've you got to say about it?"

Alice closed her locker before she spoke. She knew Lanie was really asking for advice, no matter how aggressive she sounded.

"Noemi's right. We do all have to get along in this little space," she answered slowly. "But I also heard what was going on during launch. Maybe something's bothering her. Maybe I can talk to her. But meanwhile, do us all a favor and save the fireworks for rec time, not here."

The *Santa Maria*'s rec room was the center of the ship in more ways than one.

From the streamlined outer shape of each ship, it was impossible to imagine how complex they were inside. As Dr. Al-Wahab would say, the most important thing in space *is* space. The *Santa Maria*'s inner space was a jigsaw puzzle of modular units carefully fitted into one another in the best ergonomic order.

Ergonomics was the study of how to best adapt an item of technology—whether it was a chair, a space suit, an instrument panel, or an entire spacecraft— for the human beings who would be using it. Ever since the earliest days of NASA and the Soviet cosmonaut programs, the study of ergonomics had determined how high a seat should be elevated, how loose a space suit should fit, how far the average human arm could comfortably reach to push a button or flip a switch, and even which was better—a button or a switch—for a particular function. Ergonomics affected the internal "geography" of an entire spacecraft like the *Santa Maria*.

There were the common-sense things, such as the

fact that the flying bridge should be positioned in the forward area of the ship, above the engineering section, where the communications station was. It was also obvious that the thrusters should be in the rear, with the fuel tanks a safe distance removed, but near enough so that a lot of pipes and valves and equipment weren't taking up essential space. Then there was the more complex arrangement of the engineering section, storage areas, the all-important hydroponics lab, and the sleeping quarters, so that those living and working in those areas could get where they were going without a lot of unnecessary hall traffic.

And at the very hub, or midpoint, of each ship, easiest to get to, was where people went to hang out in their down time.

Structurally, the rec room was in fact one huge, wheel-shaped room, large enough to hold the entire crew at one time. Except when one of the instructors called a briefing, however, it was subdivided like a pie chart into three distinct areas separated by clear Plexiglas "walls."

There was the commissary or, as Gen had named it, The Hub Café.

"Makes it sound less like we're eating cafeteria food," he explained, although the food consisted of the same prepackaged, freeze-dried, irradiated, rehydratable, squeeze-tube rations they were used to from Icarus.

The second area, essential in zero G even for those headed for the lesser gravity of Mars, was the gym or—thanks to Gen again—The Health Spa. Everyone was required to put in a minimum of two hours a day there, either on the ergobike or the exercise machines, or in gymnastics or aerobics, or the combination form known as astrobatics. There was also a free-play area for the usual rowdy games. Less than an hour from Earth, there was already a Spaceball match going.

Lastly, there was the area Gen called The Commons. It was where the video games were, and where Sergei was already organizing his chess club; where you went to catch up on the latest gossip, listen to music, talk, argue, get official status reports on the other two ships and all the news from Earth, and post notes on the community bulletin board if you didn't want to put them in the computer networks. Whenever there was a dispute, The Commons was where you brought it to be settled.

Which was exactly what Alice wanted Lanie and Tara to do right after Dr. Allen's general briefing.

"You all look wonderful!" was how Dr. Allen began the briefing, once everyone but Dr. Al-Wahab and the second-shift copilot had joined her in the rec room.

"We know, we know!" Sergei joked modestly. A lot of people laughed, except for the very cute girl whose attention he'd been trying to attract. Was he losing his touch?

"Right!" Dr. Allen went on when the laughter had

died down. "This won't take long, because I know you're all eager to explore a real ship after all those hours of practicing on the simulators. So, let's get down to business.

"First, you've each been assigned an A-shift or a B-shift, so let me explain the difference. Each shift is divided into twelve hours—sort of. I'll get to that part in a minute. Your twelve 'off' hours can be spent doing whatever you want, though we'd like to see you get a minimum of six to eight hours sleep somewhere in there. You all know what sleep deprivation will do to your reflexes, so I won't belabor the point.

"Your 'on' shift will either begin or end with a four-hour work/study unit in your particular field. A-shift begins with the work/study unit, B-shift ends with it. That's to give the instructors a chance at a private life too."

There was laughter at that.

"Next item: exercise. I can't stress too much the need for a minimum of two hours out of every shift, and that doesn't mean one hour one day and three hours the next, because we all know you'll get lazy and it won't happen. I know it sounds like a lot, but there are so many different forms it can take, and it has to be done. We'd like you to be mature about it and not need to be nagged, but if it comes to that, we *will* nag you. We'll also be taking a blood sample from each of you once every thirty days to make sure your blood-calcium levels are normal. Too much calcium in your blood means you're losing it from your bones, and even though Mars' gravity is only thirty-eight percent of Earth's, you don't want to be weak as kittens when we arrive."

There were nods and murmurs of agreement. Dr. Allen took a deep breath.

"Next item: housework. Everyone here is responsible for some aspect of the everyday running of the ship. We'll be posting duty rosters for kitchen chores, laundry, lab duty, especially in hydroponics, general maintenance, waste disposal—"

Everyone groaned.

"The work has to be done, people," Dr. Allen reminded them. "And in case you're interested, the instructors' names are on those rosters as well. We'll all be pulling our share."

The complaints gradually died down.

"Okay," Dr. Allen finished. "Whatever time is left over is yours for rec time. Somehow I have a feeling that a good portion of that will be devoted to Interplanetary Spaceball, but please, *please* keep those things out of the machinery!"

The laughter and wisecracks went on for several minutes.

"One final reminder," Dr. Allen said, raising one hand to get the group's attention again. "Each of your rooms has a water-usage monitor. The computers will keep an exact record of how much water each unit uses. This means that if one of you is using more than your share, your roommates will have to use less. We expect you to police one another on this. Okay, that's it. Duty rosters will be posted on the bulletin boards and in the computer 'nets'; special an-

nouncements will be made over the shipwide intercoms. If you have any questions about medical problems, see me. Anything else, speak to your team
leaders, or Dr. Berger or Dr. Al-Wahab. Any questions?"

Nathan raised his hand.

"You said at the beginning that each shift would be
divided into twelve hours, 'sort of.' Could you explain
that?"

Dr. Allen smiled at him.

"I'm glad you reminded me. During our flight we'll
be attempting to readjust our own internal clocks
from Earth time to Mars time. The Martian day, as
you know, is thirty-nine minutes and twenty-three
seconds longer than a sol, or Earth day. We've built a
program into the computers that will cumulatively
add approximately 12.44 seconds to each day, while
still keeping the digital readout at exactly 1440 minutes per day, until we reach Mars. In this way we
hope to 'reprogram' our built-in diurnal rhythms."

"Sort of like setting your watch ahead on a long
flight to avoid jet lag," someone said. "Except it usually doesn't work."

There were murmurs of agreement from almost
everyone. Some were seasoned travelers; some had
only made the journey from their hometown to one
of the five Mars training centers, but they all knew
about jet lag.

"It doesn't work when you try to add or subtract
several hours over a very short period of time," Dr.
Berger agreed, speaking for the first time. "We're

hoping that over two hundred twenty days our internal clocks will barely feel the difference of a few seconds added each day."

Dr. Berger had been silent throughout Dr. Allen's briefing. He had been lounging—if it was possible to lounge in zero G—near the video games, watching and listening. Now that he had everyone's attention, he straightened his lanky body, ran his long fingers through his bright red beard, and cleared his throat.

"Similar experiments have been done with plants," he explained in his Israeli accent. "We've been able to change their 'thinking' about time, despite the fact that, on the evolutionary scale, they're far older than we are."

"So if we're as smart as plants, we should have no worries," Alice chimed in softly.

She didn't know what had made her conquer her usual shyness and speak up. She would be Dr. Berger's chief assistant in the hydroponics lab, and was trying to overcome her nervousness around him. She didn't know why Dr. Berger made her nervous, but he did. He was doing that now, just by smiling at her.

"Let's hope so, Alice," he said.

Dr. Allen's watch beeped. It was 1100 hours.

"Will we have to turn our watches in, since we can't match their programs with the computers?" Sergei wanted to know.

"Someone should invent a Mars-time watch!" Gen suggested.

"If you do, the patent's yours!" Dr. Allen said. "No,

you don't have to turn in your watches. Just be aware that they won't be accurate once we get to Mars. Okay, briefing's over. We'll be entering lunar orbit in about forty-nine hours from now, and we'll have the E.V.A. cameras out for a last look. That's it!"

There was a lot of milling around, some jostling near the duty rosters as people checked to see what chores they'd been assigned and when. Sergei began collecting the members of his newly formed chess club. Soon the rec room was half empty. The Plexiglas dividers had been slid back into place, and some people were already working out in the Health Spa. Alice looked around for Tara, but she was already gone.

Chapter Three

"Now, if we had enough fuel for 'constant boost' technology"—Karl was lecturing Nathan as they entered The Commons—"we could create artificial gravity on a ship this size and avoid the pitfalls of zero G entirely. Perhaps someday we could even modulate it between Earth and Mars so as to gradually acclimate ourselves to Mars gravity."

"Karl is dreaming again!" Sergei remarked, glancing up from the chessboard, where he had his opponent's king in jeopardy. "As it happens, my friend, we do not yet have this technology. Some of us, however, do not mind."

Sergei floated cross-legged in midair, the chessboard hovering between him and a boy with spiked hair, two earrings in his left earlobe and a tattoo on one arm. The chess pieces had magnets on the bottom to stick them to the board, but the game and its players could drift in freefall anywhere around The Commons, which was exactly what Sergei had in mind. There were three girls he hadn't yet met having their meal break very near the Plexiglas partition of The Hub Café. The one in the middle waved and giggled every time Sergei drifted past, and she had the most gorgeous smile.

"Gives him something else to fuss about!" the boy with the spikes remarked without turning around, scowling at his predicament on the chessboard. "Ol' Sieggie's still walkin' about with his Velcro stuck tight. The bloke ain't flexible."

Anyone working in engineering had to use the Velcro panels to keep from drifting too close to hazardous machinery, but most people free-floated everywhere else. Not Karl. He used his Velcro-heeled slippers whenever he wasn't in the copilot's chair, working his way doggedly, step by step, wherever he had to go.

"Some of us are airheads, and some of us prefer to keep our feet on the ground!" Karl addressed the back of the punker's head. "And my name is not Sieggie."

Oh, brother! Nathan thought. Here comes World War III.

"Hey, guys . . ." he began, but neither Karl nor the punker was listening. Think fast! he thought. "Um, I was hoping one of you would explain this 'constant boost' thing to me. I must have been catching some Z's during that part of physics."

That should work, Nathan thought. Nothing makes two people stop fighting like the chance to show off for a third person. But why do I always have to be the peacemaker?

"Constant-boost flight is not difficult to understand," Karl began, settling himself unsteadily on Sergei's side of the board to study the game. Unstuck from his Velcro, he wasn't that sure of himself. "The rocketry we have today enables us to use fuel only at the beginning and end of an interplanetary journey. For the rest of the time we allow inertia to carry us through space. That is why it will take us over seven months to get to Mars . . ."

"Checkmate!" Sergei announced pleasantly.

The punker studied the board, saw no way out.

"I give!" he said, tipping his king over to resign.

"Another?" Sergei invited him.

"Nah, you and Sieggie play this one. I'll watch."

"Someday we will have rockets that function on the principle of constant acceleration," Karl continued, ignoring the punker. "A ship would accelerate at a constant thrust of point one G until midpoint, then flip over so that it is actually going backward, and decelerate at point one G until it arrived at its destination. . . ."

Nathan nodded, half listening. He was studying the punker, trying to read him. Now that he had lost the chess game, he had pushed himself away from the board as if leaning back in an invisible chair, and folded his arms across his chest. Nathan noticed that he had ripped the sleeves out of his coveralls to show off his tattoo. He had further personalized his gear by wearing biker's gloves—the backless, fingerless, covered-with-studs kind, and biker's boots, even though hard footwear was a hazard in zero G. In addition to the small gold ring and the diamond studs,

37

he wore a heavy gold chain with a crucifix which kept floating out of the collar of his coveralls. Whenever it did, he would shove it back in again to keep it from hitting him in the face. Who was he trying to be anyway? Nathan wondered.

". . . And as a consequence," Karl went on, setting up his pieces on the chessboard. Sergei was waving at the girl in the café again. "Not only would we enjoy a constant normal gravity, but it would take us less than five days to reach Mars."

"Five *days*?" Nathan repeated. Maybe he hadn't been paying attention.

"Even so," Karl finished, moving his queen's pawn, though his steely blue eyes were not on the chessboard, but locked with the punker's, "there are people like Ian McShane, who will always be late for their shift."

The punker glanced at the nearest digital display and groaned.

"Sister Mary Frances, Sieggie! Whyn't you tell me?"

He spun into a fancy backflip to impress the girls in the café, then propelled himself through the rec room door, colliding with a sleepy Gen.

"Sorry, mate!" Ian muttered, rocketing away.

"No problem!" Gen yawned. He was useless until he'd had his morning tea.

"Dr. Allen holds a special briefing for the copilot trainees at the start of every workshift," Karl said, nodding toward the departing Ian with a gleam of satisfaction in his eye. "If Ian continues to be late,

Dr. Allen may take him off the copilot roster."

"You could have told him what time it was," Nathan offered in Ian's defense.

"He could learn to be more disciplined!" Karl shot back.

Nathan looked at Sergei, expecting him to say something. The Russian boy glanced up from the chessboard with a knight in his hand and shrugged. Life was too short to waste on trivia.

"You should be more careful of Ian McShane, Karl my friend," Sergei warned, moving his knight. "Rumor has it he almost joined the IRA before he was recruited for the Mars program."

"I am quaking in my Velcro!" Karl remarked, not realizing he had made a joke until both of his friends went quietly hysterical on him. "Laugh all you want, Sergei my friend. I have your queen in jeopardy."

Sergei gawked at the chessboard. *"Bozhe moi! You're getting better!"*

"The Irish Republican Army?" Alice repeated when Lanie told her. "I can't believe that!"

"Believe it," Lanie said. "I was running Tara White's file, and I—sort of got curious."

"I don't think it's right for you to be going through personnel files, either," Alice said primly.

She and Lanie had just come offshift. Tara and Lisette were already on. Noemi, as usual, was still in the shower.

"Look," Lanie said, running her hands through her

hair. It was almost completely grown out to its soft blond natural color again, and it looked terrific; she wondered why she'd ever gone platinum. "Computers are my field. Dr. Al-Wahab says I'm the best he's ever seen. That means I'm fast, and I'm accurate. There's only so much incoming data for me to process, so many functions for me to check on. The ship does the rest. So since I have to be at the keyboard for four hours anyway, and the data files are there anyway—"

"And you're also the best hacker any of us has ever seen," Alice added.

She wished she were as talented as Lanie, but then, her talents lay elsewhere. She was fussing with a small planter, where she'd started some pumpkin seeds in a hydroponic nutrient base. It had been her idea to start planters in the sleeping quarters as well as in the hydroponics lab. They would add to the oxygen supply while they brightened up the place. Dr. Berger had raised his eyebrows in surprise when she suggested it, and Alice had expected him to say no.

What he said was: "Brilliant. Wish I'd thought of it. By all means—go right ahead."

"Well . . ." Lanie said modestly. "Do you want to know what I found out or don't you?"

Even Alice couldn't resist juicy gossip.

"I suppose we'd get along better if we knew more about one another," she admitted, finishing with the planter and putting her tools back in their zippered belt pouch. "And since Tara's so close-mouthed when she's with us . . ."

40

"Okay, here it is." Lanie stuck her heels to the wall so she could wave her hands around without flying all over the room.

"Tara's the same as us, from Harlem, in New York City, a project kid, like me. She went to some fancy technical school called Bronx High School of Science after acing the entry exam and interviews. She wrote for the newspaper, even did some videos that won awards. Her family's pretty big, two brothers and two sisters. Her mom's a day care teacher and her dad a school custodian. And guess her favorite sport?"

Alice shrugged. "Tennis?"

"Yeah, right. With her legs? She's a girls' basketball star. She even got offered college scholarships for it, but decided on our program instead.

"What's her specialty?"

"That's what's weird. It's communications. Writing, TV, videos—stuff like that. Not a techie whiz like the rest of us, right?" Lanie made a face and Alice laughed.

"Maybe that's why she's so sensitive. Good to know."

"As for Ian, he's the seventh of nine kids. One older brother was killed by a British soldier in Belfast, another one's in jail for planting a bomb in a restaurant for revenge. Ian would've ended up the same way, only a priest in his grade school saw how good he was in math and practically beat him into studying and getting top grades and applying for the Mars program in high school. Otherwise he would've ended up in prison too. Or dead."

41

Both girls heard the shower stop, and knew Noemi would be out soon, toweling her hair, letting her clothes float all over the place.

"You can't have gotten all that from the regulation files," Alice said carefully. "There isn't that much in them. You know that."

"And you know I'm the best hacker you've ever seen." Lanie grinned modestly. "You just said so."

Alice's eyes widened. "You got into classified files? Lanie, that's impossible!"

"It is not," Lanie said. "Our database is linked to the Mission Control databases on Icarus and on Earth. There's a time lag, but I can get into any system they have. There are newspaper clippings on microfiche, just like the ones in the ship's 'library.' "

"You're good!" Alice shook her head. "I'm glad you're on our side!"

On the third day out the moon filled the entire E.V.A. screen, and the view from the flying bridge was awesome. It was Dr. Al-Wahab, taking his turn at piloting the *Santa Maria*, who made the announcement.

"Ladies and gentlemen. . . " Even over the ship-wide intercom, Dr. Al-Wahab's voice was never above a whisper. ". . . welcome to the moon."

There were no words to describe it. Every culture on Earth had some legend associated with this mysterious natural satellite. Whether it was the man in the moon or a dog or a goddess, the tree of life or a dragon nibbling at the edges to cause the phases, there was something awesome about this shining hunk of rock.

"Luna, Diana, Selene, Phoebe, Cynthia, Artemis, Hecate, Astarte . . ." Karl recited all of the moon's many names. When nobody paid attention, he started pointing out landmarks. "There is the Sea of Tranquility, *Mare Spumans* or the Foaming Sea, *Mare Moscoviense—*"

"Shut up, Karl!" Lanie whispered, too awed to speak out loud.

"Where we're going, we'll have two moons," Lisette reminded them. "Phobos and Deimos are a lot smaller than the moon we're used to, but . . ."

Somehow Nathan's team had gravitated—anti-gravitated might be more accurate—together to stare at the image on the E.V.A. screen. Nathan felt Sergei slip between him and Lisette, a hand on each of their shoulders.

"We haven't talked together, just the three of us," the Russian boy said, watching the video screen so he wouldn't get embarrassed. "But I'll admit now I made a fool of myself back on Icarus."

"Is that an apology?" Lisette snapped, shrugging Sergei's hand off her shoulder.

"Sure it is," Nathan said before Sergei could say anything. "As far as we're concerned, it never happened."

The two boys exchanged high-fives. Lisette sulked for a moment, until Sergei kissed her cheek, as if she were his sister.

"So many girls, so little time!" Sergei shrugged. "Sometimes I get carried away."

Nathan felt relieved. He also felt depressed. Once the moon was behind them, there would be nothing but empty space between them and Mars. It was enough to give anyone a hollow feeling in the pit of his stomach.

They'd talked about acrophobia, the fear of heights, while they were on Icarus. Everyone had been assigned E.V.A. work during the construction of the three ships. First they'd practiced in simulators, then they'd gone out into actual space, sometimes with a restraint tether, like the ones the Apollo crews had used while working outside the lunar modules, sometimes with thruster boots for better maneuverability.

"Don't look down" might work for sky-diving or rock-climbing. It didn't work for deep space work because there *was* no down. Several candidates had been eliminated from the Mars program because they couldn't overcome their fear of working in vacuum, with nothing under them.

"If you want to get technical about it," Gen had said once in a philosophical mood, "our whole lives are spent in space. You may think you've got a solid floor or solid ground under you, but even Earth is just a speck floating out there in all that nothing. The odds against its ever being knocked out of orbit are low, but—"

"Gen!" everyone had shouted him down.

"Hey, it could happen!"

They'd all had a case of the shudders after that conversation. Gen could be a real pain, especially when he was right. It didn't seem to bother him. He wrote a song that night called "Nothing but Space," and spent the next three days setting it to different guitar riffs.

So we're really no worse off inside a spaceship than we would be on Earth, Nathan thought. Yeah, right!

He drifted down the almost-empty corridors, passing little knots of people staring at the moon on the video monitors at their work stations or wherever they happened to be. He had this sudden need to be alone. But where could you be alone with all these people?

Nathan stopped at the "radio room," which wasn't a room so much as a corner of Engineering Ops, where messages came in from the two other ships, from Mission Control, and from private Earth transmissions. Sometimes people got "personal mail"—long distance messages from friends and family on Earth.

"Nothing for you, Long," the girl at the Ops station reported, checking her message board, then seeing the look on his face. "Sorry!"

"No problem," Nathan said.

He hadn't expected his mother to be able to send messages very often; they were more expensive than long distance phone calls. Sometimes there was a long wait to get around interference and other people's stacked-up messages. Nathan told himself it didn't matter. But it did.

He had more than an hour of downshift time before his exercise stint. He decided he would go back to his room and read for a while, even though he knew Karl would probably be there, and he didn't feel much like talking.

Instead, he ended up sticking one Velcro wristband to a wall panel and wiping a tear off his eyelashes.

He hadn't cried since he was ten. No, that wasn't true. He'd cried when his father moved out, after the divorce. But that was important; you were allowed to cry over important things. Crying because you were leaving Earth and the moon behind and your best friend had just apologized for making a move on your girl and it all made you homesick was pretty weak. Nathan hoped no one saw him.

Someone did. She grabbed his arm.

"You too, huh?"

"Me too, what?" Nathan looked Alice straight in the eye and tried to bluff. "Must've gotten some dust in my eye or something."

"Oh, sure!" Alice said. Nathan looked at her again and saw that she had tears in both eyes and wasn't pretending. "We're supposed to be the strong ones. You and me. Not supposed to lose our cool like the rest of 'em. Well, I get bloody sick of it sometimes!"

She wiped her eyes on her hands, wiped her hands on her coveralls. Nathan put his arms around her.

"I'm not feeling very strong right now either," he said.

"Thanks!" Alice sniffled, hugging him back. They both let go before anyone saw. "Better find a hanky.

46

Can't let my nose run in zero G."

"Yuk!" Nathan agreed. Where they were crying a minute ago, now they were laughing hysterically.

"Now I've got tears in my eyes for a different reason!" Alice wheezed, catching her breath. She punched Nathan on the arm. "You're a pal, Nathan Long. Thanks again!"

"No problem!" Nathan gasped, still winded from laughing himself. "You're a good friend too, Alice."

He wanted to add: I've never had a sister, but if I did, I think I'd like her to be like you.

"See you around, Nate," Alice said, punching his arm again.

Lanie yanked her into their roomette as she passed.

"Take a look at this!" she said, jabbing a finger at the water meter. "She's over her limit again. And she's still in there!"

Alice was still thinking about Nathan, and had no idea what Lanie was talking about at first.

"What do you mean, she's still in there?"

"Noemi!" Lanie exploded, waving her hands at the shower unit, where the In Use light was on, and they could hear the hiss of the pressurized water. "Tell me, have you seen her anywhere but in the shower lately?"

Chapter Four

"When I was small . . ." Noemi explained, combing out her still-wet hair, "whenever I fell down and hurt myself or was feeling very sad, our housekeeper, Flora, would draw me a nice hot bath. She would scent it with Mama's imported French bath salts, and I would soak for hours . . ."

"How nice!" Lanie said sarcastically.

"It always cheered me up!" Noemi argued. "I may not have a hot bath again for three years, but there is something about water, about being clean and knowing that you smell nice—excuse me, but I need that!"

"You've used more than your limit every day since we've left," Alice said quietly. Lanie had been keeping records.

"The recovery system is still inefficient!" Noemi snapped back. "I'll bet you if I could have a go at the computers long enough to work on the theoretical model, I could improve the system by another fifteen percent."

"You can't get that much computer time," Lanie

started to say. "You know we're on time share—"

"But you can get enough time for your gossip and poking into other people's files!" Noemi accused her.

"The point is, you can't use this much water under the system we have," Alice said with a warning look at Lanie to just keep quiet. "In the meantime—"

"In the meantime they have assigned me kitchen duty!" Noemi protested. "Kitchen duty, as if I were a servant! There is no use for my brilliance in mathematics so far, so they have me shoving meals into microwave ovens and disposing of empty containers. I broke two fingernails on this last shift alone—"

"Aww!" Lanie said in mock-sympathy.

"We're sorry for you, Noemi," Alice said. "But suppose all of us felt the same way? Suppose all five of us in this room felt depressed and needed a hot shower at the same time?"

Noemi seemed surprised that anyone could possibly feel what she was feeling. "I never thought about that," she said honestly.

She hadn't thought of other people's feelings, hadn't thought of anything at all since takeoff except why, oh why had she ever applied to the To Mars Together program? True, she had been so horribly bored with her old life that she would do anything to get away. Now she wasn't so sure.

Life for a girl of her social class was an endless round of parties and invitations. It was the nuisance of fending off one boy after another because one or both of her parents wouldn't consider him "suitable." The ones her parents did find suitable were the ones

Noemi found the most boring. Being the daughter of wealthy parents had placed social obligations upon her that her two friends couldn't imagine. She had had to escape, to keep from being smothered to death.

But what had she escaped to? She couldn't change her mind until the orbits of Mars and Earth were close again. Three years from now. She wouldn't ride the horses up into the hills again, nor hear the birds calling in the woods at the back of her family's property, or see her parents, her sisters, and Flora again. Forget about a long hot bath.

Tears flowed down Noemi's cheeks, and she dashed them angrily away.

"You're picking on me!" she shouted. "You're ganging up on me, and I won't stand for it! None of you knows what I'm going through, none of you!"

"Maybe you should talk to someone who does," Alice suggested. "Dr. Allen's a trained psychologist. Maybe—"

"Oh, right! You think it's as simple as that, do you?" Noemi left her hairbrush floating in midair, slipped her long hair into a fancy barrette—it was even beginning to get on *her* nerves—and pushed out of the roomette, leaving her clothes, her towel, and the hairbrush floating toward the air vents.

"This is more serious than I thought," Alice said.

"You know it!" Lanie agreed, pulling Noemi's belongings out of thin air and stuffing them into her sleep-sack. "She's a worse slob than I thought!"

"Now is when the hard times begin," Dr. Berger said half aloud.

Alice looked across a row of snap peas at Tara, who frowned. Was Dr. Berger talking to them, to himself, or to the plants?

Tara and Alice worked the same shift in the hydroponics lab. It was the only place on the ship that had gravity, an artificial one created by constantly rotating the lab to create enough centrifugal force to maintain a Mars-equivalent gravity.

While it was true that plants were photosensitive, growing toward the light, Dr. Berger didn't want to take any chances. Plants that spent too much of their growing time without gravity, he had discovered, tended to grow roots and stems at random, and didn't flourish. Besides, if the current crop of plants could be started in .38G, the agronomists would know how they would behave in Mars gravity before they got to Mars.

Whoever worked in the lab tended to get tired more readily than those working without gravity, but they also suffered less calcium loss, and were excused from some of the mandatory two-hour exercise. After they'd been under way for a few weeks, volunteers began to arrive, hoping to get out of some exercise routines as well. Getting in and out of the lab turned out to be more of an athletic feat than they had bargained for.

First you had to wait for the rotation to bring one of the lab's hatchways into range. Then you had to jump in quickly, feet first, as if you were sky-diving. And the transition from zero G to .38 was like stepping off a suddenly-stopped escalator.

"Scary!" Tara remarked the first time she tried it. Alice had had to catch her to keep her from knocking over several trays of seedlings. She'd expected Tara to be furious with her for even touching her. But she was surprisingly easy to get along with as long as Lanie wasn't around. She got along well with everyone in the lab, including Dr. Berger.

Dr. Berger wasn't the authority figure they'd expected. He treated his trainees the way he treated his plants—with a great deal of patience and absolutely no favoritism.

"Plants are easier than people," he told his trainees on their first day. "Biologically complex but psychologically simple. Does anyone know why?"

Most of them looked at him as if he'd suddenly gone whacko, but Alice understood.

"They eat and drink what they're told, and don't have sulks or temper tantrums," she offered.

"Exactly!" Dr. Berger had smiled, making her blush, not for the first time.

"We do know that plants have nervous systems," he went on. "They react to pain as well as to auditory stimuli—music, and the human voice. That's why I will be playing classical music for them at all times. Not rock, I'm afraid; it gives them migraines." The trainees laughed nervously, not sure if he was serious. "You will also hear me talking to them, and I encourage you to do the same. Or just talk to one another. The plants will love it, and you'll get to know each other better. If nothing else, the increased CO_2 levels will help."

"Roger, *Pinta*, we copy that." Gen spoke crisply into his transmitter, his nimble fingers playing over the communications board. "Keep your ears on. We will repeat transmission at 0800. That's a ten-four. *Santa Maria*, out."

He flipped the comm toggle and the idiot light went out. He took off the headset, shook out his long, silky black hair, and rubbed his hands together, laughing out loud.

"I love this job!" he announced. "It's so professional—so real. Just like in the movies. Did you hear me? Do I sound professional or what? 'Roger, *Pinta*, we copy that. Hailing frequencies open.' I love it!"

Gen was a natural on capcom. He was as much at ease talking to Mission Control—even with the time lag that occurred as they traveled farther from Earth—as he was interfacing with the two sister ships. The three ships kept up a regular communication every hour on the hour, to report on headway, check relative distance, double-check times and trajectories, and generally keep each other company in the big, dark emptiness of space. Gen had transformed what could have been a boring job into deejay heaven. When he wasn't running ordinary comm, he played his favorite music, and any he could borrow from his crewmates, over the *Santa Maria*'s intercom. He'd even named his new radio station SNAP.

"For *Santa Maria, Nina* and *Pinta*," he explained. "Radio SNAP. Snap! I love it!"

"You love this job?" Lisette asked him, shoving a systems-check clipboard at him. "Good! Now do the rest of it!"

"Systems check!" Gen groaned, clutching the clipboard to his heart. "Three hundred idiot lights to check to see if they read off or on. Seventy-three frequency bands to be fine-tuned. Four thousand six hundred ninety-three circuit boards to be tested and retested—"

"Twenty-four idiot lights, ten frequency bands, and I've never counted the circuit boards," Lisette said mercilessly. "Stop exaggerating."

"Borrring!" Gen replied, transforming the clipboard into an air guitar and playing an impressive Clapton riff.

"Boring or not, you'd better have it done by 0800," Lisette said, trying not to crack up at Gen's performance.

"I'm thinking of growing a mustache for the midpoint ceremonies," Gen mused, rubbing his naked upper lip. "I hear the secretary general of the United Nations is going to make a speech, and we'll be on all the media. Live interviews between us and all the heads of state of Earth. D'you think I'd look good with a mustache?"

Lisette just snorted in disbelief.

Nathan and Sergei were in engineering running the E.V.A. cameras. This job was boredom personified. Every centimeter of the *Santa Maria*'s outer hull that could be picked up within camera range had to be scanned for irregularities or possible damage from dust or space debris. The smallest scratch or meteor dent would register on camera if you were quick enough to see it. The computer system would register major problems—a comm system going out, a sealant leak, any unexplained temperature or pressure falloff—but the small stuff required human eyes and human brains. One blink, one yawn, one daydream, and you could miss something that might endanger the entire ship.

Two crew members at a time were assigned to watch the monitors for an hour per shift. There was nothing to relieve the boredom of staring at meter after meter of stark white hull, shadowless in the sun's unobscured glare, except where the comm equipment or the now-extended solar wings created shadows darker than dark. Dr. Al-Wahab was strict about idle chatter; too much talk meant you weren't paying attention to your monitor.

"Lanie saw the E.V.A. roster," Sergei whispered anyway, always one to bend the rules. "She and I are first out in the hardsuits, day after next."

"Huh?" Nathan was beginning to get a headache just behind his eyes; he wasn't paying attention. "Say again? Didn't hear you."

"Lanie and I will be going E.V.A. to do hands-on backup checks, day after next," Sergei repeated. Even his whisper conveyed his excitement. Every ten days, a team of two from engineering would be out in space, checking the outside of the ship. "We're ahead of the *Nina* and *Pinta* and making good time. Lanie and I will be the first humans ever to go out in space this far from Earth."

Nathan looked up over his monitor, making sure Sergei was still watching his.

"Really? That's fantastic. Congratulations. But it's bogus, isn't it? Each team after you will get to go farther out."

Sergei looked over his monitor at Nathan as Nathan instinctively looked down.

"There's still the honor of being first, no?" Sergei wondered if Nathan was jealous.

He was. He had wanted to be the first to go E.V.A. He couldn't help wondering if this was some political thing, some decision made by the powers on Earth. A Russian and an American in space together looked real good for the media. Very political, very now—just like the Apollo/Salyut mission all those years ago.

But Lanie was a computer specialist—why pick her? Was it because she was one of Dr. Al-Wahab's favorites, and a girl too? The feminist angle always made good headlines and sound bites. But what good was a computer specialist out on a tether in space? For that matter, Sergei was a geologist. Why not save him for when they got near the asteroids, and let an astrophysics specialist—like me, Nathan thought—go first?

Nathan had been pestering Dr. Al-Wahab to let him take readings on some of the nearer stars when it was his turn to go E.V.A., readings more accurate than they could get on Earth.

Dr. Al-Wahab had smiled his gentle smile, which didn't mean he was going to give in.

"We'll see, Nathan. For now, we have the Canopus lock to help us navigate, and that's all we need the stars for, practically speaking. When you go E.V.A., you will have enough oxygen for only two hours. Enough time to assure the safety of the ship, not for elaborate experiments. We'll see."

So that was that. Nathan squinted at his monitor, trying to remember the biofeedback technique for getting rid of a headache. There wasn't one for getting rid of jealousy.

"That's the trouble with you rich-kid science nerds," Ian McShane was saying, running checks on the co-pilot's station. "You don't know nothin' about world events, and you couldn't care less. You sit there with your noses in front of a screen your whole lives—"

"I am not a science nerd!" Karl said stiffly from the pilot's chair. He couldn't say much about the "rich-kid" part; compared to the poverty Ian had grown up with, his own family had been—well—comfortable. "And I am aware of world events."

"Flashes on the telly!" Ian snorted. "You don't understand the people end of it. You watch the troubles in Belfast and you think: It's just a bunch of punks throwing rocks at soldiers. You don't understand what's behind it."

Dr. Allen listened to the two boys squabbling from the "ready room"—a tiny alcove off the flying bridge just big enough to curl up for a nap. She'd given Karl his first chance in the pilot's seat. They were in open space, the dangers were minimal, the ship was largely on autopilot, and she was inches away if there was a problem. Naturally Ian was envious. They'd been sniping at each other, by Dr. Allen's watch, for nearly an hour now.

Should she break it up?

Nah, she thought. Let them get it out of their systems!

"You ever hot-wire a car?" Ian was asking.

"Certainly not!" Karl retorted.

"Ever defuse a bomb?"

Karl narrowed his eyes at the Irish boy. "And you have, I suppose?"

Ian nodded. "If it's mechanical, I can strip it down and reassemble it before you can blink. If it's broke, Ian McShane can fix it!"

Braggart! Karl thought, but managed not to say it out loud. He was enjoying his chance to fly the ship, and he wasn't going to let a punk like McShane ruin it for him.

"Aiee!" Noemi shrieked as the bag of uncooked rice she'd been opening slipped out of her hand.

Several thousand grains of rice flew all over the

58

kitchen area. Noemi would be picking them out of the air one at a time for hours. She began cursing and crying at the same time.

People's nerves seemed to be getting frayed all over the ship. Maybe that was what Dr. Berger had meant about the hard times, Alice thought.

"Ow, *watch* it!" a boy named Jhong yelled from two rows over.

"Sorry!" came a voice from the far side of the hydroponics lab's curved deck. Jhong picked up the trowel that had nearly clipped his ear off and shook it angrily at the boy who had dropped it.

The weird thing about working in gravity again, even if it was only 38 percent of Earth's, was that you had to learn all over again about dropping things.

For months on Icarus and weeks now on the *Santa Maria,* they'd mastered the art of letting things float at hand, clipping them to a belt loop, or sticking them to a convenient Velcro wall panel. It was conditioned reflex to let go of something and expect to find it floating nearby the next time you needed it. It seemed unnatural somehow to watch something plummet out of reach, and possibly become a dangerous projectile as soon as it left your hand.

"It's okay, dears, don't worry!" Alice soothed the plants she was tending. She'd taken Dr. Berger's advice about talking to them.

Dr. Berger certainly did his share. In addition to the endless CDs of Beethoven, Liszt, and Mozart he played constantly, he pottered among the soybean seedlings, the fruit trees, the pumpkins and legumes and herbs, talking to his charges all the time. Most of his trainees were content to talk to one another and let the plants eavesdrop; it was too weird to talk to something that couldn't talk back. Only Alice and Tara talked directly *to* the plants.

"My great-grandmother owned a pig farm on some of the poorest land in Georgia," Tara said one afternoon. Alice noticed she kept her eyes on the plants as she fed them. She's really very shy, for all her showing off in quarters, Alice thought. "She also grew cotton to earn a little extra income. Some winters, it kept her family from starving."

"I've never seen a cotton plant," Alice said.

"Yeah, neither have I. I've never even been on a farm."

"My family has a sheep ranch in New Zealand," Alice said. She had a sudden vision of Bobby and the twins, and thought of how big they must be growing. Their lives were going on without her.

"You must miss them." Tara watched the emotions racing across Alice's plain face. "What do you miss most? If you don't mind my asking."

"I don't mind!" Alice tossed one of her practical braids back over her shoulder. "What I miss most is lambing time. My dad and I used to sit up all night sometimes if one of the ewes was having trouble. Why are baby lambs always born at dawn, I wonder. The sun would just be peeping through the slats of the barn door, and out it would come — all wet and

60

wobbly, stick legs struggling to stand."

Alice looked down at her hands, remembering the feel of lambs' wool.

"There won't be anything alive on Mars at all until we get there. "Except maybe microbes, Dr. Berger says," Tara said.

"But we'll be able to raise chickens someday," Alice added, cheering herself up. "Dr. Berger says the next wave of pioneers will bring fertilized eggs with them. Chickens and ducks and maybe even geese and swans . . . Of course, chickens aren't the same as lambs," Alice said, tying up her bean runners again.

"No, I guess they're not," Tara agreed.

Something went *clang*, and one of the boys nearby howled in pain; he'd dropped a pair of pruning shears on his own foot. The two girls looked at each other and burst out laughing.

Chapter Five

No one knew how it started. No one actually organized it. But the word got around. If you had a problem or a complaint, needed advice or just a chance to shoot the bull, you somehow found yourself in The Commons during the two-hour time slot that straddled the end of B-shift and the beginning of A-shift.

Sometimes there were only two or three people gathered together, sometimes a whole crowd. There was no official meeting, no Robert's Rules of Order, and no one seemed to be in charge. The adults aboard never made an appearance unless they were invited. And while there might be a lot of shouting and time wasted, somehow things got settled most of the time.

What was weird was that the same kind of communal bull sessions sprang up in the same time slot aboard the *Nina* and the *Pinta* as well. No one organized these either. They just sort of happened.

Personal messages could pass between ships only when the capcom channels were free of more important communications. One such message had gotten through to Sergei, and he'd been sweating it out ever since.

"I am in deep trouble!" he announced as he and Nathan completed an hour-long session on the ergobikes and rounded off their exercise unit with astrobatics and three rousing sets of Spaceball.

Nathan handed Sergei a towel, wiping sweat from his own face. "What's up?"

"You remember I told you about Ludmilla?"

"From Star City? The one you went to school with in Leningrad?"

"The same." Sergei swallowed hard. "On Icarus, Lanie checked the files and found Ludmilla was rostered on the *Nina*. Somehow, she found out my comm code. I've just gotten a message from her."

"Gee, Sergei, that's gr—" Nathan started to say, then saw the stricken look on his friend's face. "Oh, man, not again!"

Sergei nodded miserably.

"I must explain that it was always far more serious on her part than on mine. It was she who decided we were boyfriend and girlfriend, not I. And while I am still very fond of her—"

"You don't want to be tied down," Nathan finished for him.

"Not only that—" Sergei swallowed again—"it seems Ludmilla and Raisa were in many of the same classes at Star City. Do I have to tell you that my name often came into the conversation?"

63

"So they've been comparing notes, and found out you were leading them both on. . . ." Nathan just shook his head. "And as soon as we land, Ludmilla will be gunning for you. Man, you are impossible! If all the girls you ever knew came after you at the same time . . ."

"They would tear him to pieces!" Karl huffed from the far corner.

He finished his own exercise, a peculiar form of mid-air lap swimming he had designed himself, and caught up with his friends, a little red in the face but in great shape as always.

Sergei grinned at the German boy.

"So many girls, so little time!" he said, not for the first time.

"If I had a girl," Karl stated, wiping his sweating face and draping the towel around his neck, "I would treat her with more respect. I would not be as indifferent to her feelings as you are."

"Have you ever had a steady girl?" Sergei asked, never shy about asking personal questions.

"No one steady, no," Karl said too quickly, thinking of a certain raven-haired, freckled-faced Alsatian girl named Hanni, an exchange student at his school for a year, just long enough to break his heart. "I was always too busy with my studies."

"He's a lone wolf," Gen chimed in. Somehow they had drifted into The Commons, and somehow Gen had simply popped up in their midst. "Just like me."

"You are always making too much noise for any

girl to get near you!" Karl said, teasing in his dry way.

It was true. When Gen and his guitar weren't plugged in somewhere, Gen and his radio station, or Gen and his portable disc player were. Or he was playing riffs on his air guitar and singing at the top of his lungs. He'd been kicked out of the roomette he shared with Nathan, Karl, and Sergei more than once. Except that there didn't seem to be anywhere else for him to play.

Which was the very first topic on the gripe list at today's bull session.

"— Noise pollution!" a girl named Cathy was saying as Nathan and his friends joined the crowd. "We should have a rule about loud talking in the sleeping quarters during offshifts. I mean, if you want to party, come here. Go to The Hub, or even hang out in the labs, for crying out loud."

"No, please, our poor plants!" Alice said, getting a laugh.

"All right, you see what I'm saying," Cathy said. "But when people are trying to sleep, there shouldn't be any loud talking. As for music—"

She glared at Gen.

"I'm not mentioning any names, but someone's been mouthing off on the radio station about forming a rock group. As if he didn't make enough noise all by himself!"

All eyes were on Gen.

"May I talk now?" he asked calmly. "I mean, for

65

someone who's complaining about noise pollution—"

"Now, wait a minute—!" Cathy started to say, but there were murmurs of "Let him talk!" "Yeah, it's his turn!"

Gen slipped his hands into his coverall pockets, very cool.

"I'm sorry about the noise, but without my music I'd just plain go crazy. Sometimes there's a song in my head and it just has to come out. If there were a definite place I could practice, fine. But when I come in here, there are people talking or playing games or listening to their own music; I don't want to get in their way. So what's left? I'm open to suggestions."

"We'll work something out!" Nathan said suddenly, not at all sure what or how.

"Dr. Al-Wahab, I can't!" Lanie protested. "I can't tell you why, but I just can't do it, okay?"

The ship's engineer looked puzzled. His best pupil was never shy about what she could or couldn't do. It was her ability to take calculated risks that was most interesting about her. Why was she so nervous about going E.V.A.?

"I will replace you with someone else if you like," Dr. Al-Wahab said. "But I don't understand why you're so reluctant. It isn't as if you don't know the work."

"It isn't that," Lanie said, avoiding his eyes. "It's

66

the TV coverage! If it were just Sergei and me doing our job, no problem. But knowing everyone on Earth is watching—I can't deal with that!"

Dr. Al-Wahab continued to frown. "You are shy about the TV coverage? You, of all people! I thought you would be thrilled. Won't your family be proud?"

"I have no family!" Lanie shouted. Some of the people in engineering had stopped what they were doing to stare at her. She lowered her voice. "I mean, there's just my mother and—well—she's an alcoholic and—I wouldn't want the TV people bothering her. It could be—embarrassing."

Dr. Al-Wahab looked thoughtful for a moment. "I didn't realize that. I'm sorry. I will choose someone else, if you're sure."

"I'm sure!" Lanie snapped, then went back to her computer keyboard.

It was some minutes before she was calm enough to work. She thought she'd escaped the mess she left behind on Earth, but she was wrong. It was following her, even out in space.

"I didn't know you played chess," Sergei said, surprised when Lisette asked him for a game.

"There's a lot about me you don't know," the dark-haired girl said. "A lot of things you never bothered to find out. Can I ask you something?"

Sergei hesitated. Was this more girl trouble?

"Sure," he said.

"Nathan wants very much to go E.V.A. with you, doesn't he? To be part of the first team in deep space."

"Yes, but Lanie—"

"Lanie's not going," Lisette said. "No one knows why, but she asked Dr. Al-Wahab to take her name off the roster."

I know why, Sergei thought. Our whole team knows why, at least the original seven, but we agreed not to tell anyone else.

"And?" he asked casually, studying the chessboard.

"And my name came up next. Apparently it's some sort of random computer-selection thing. So nobody can say it isn't fair. And I was thinking . . ."

"You were thinking of stepping aside because Nathan is next on the roster," Sergei finished for her. He castled, and waited for her to make her next move.

"Something like that."

"That's very noble of you," Sergei said sincerely.

Lisette frowned at the chessboard. If she didn't plan her next move carefully, she could lose her queen.

"I wouldn't say 'noble.' It doesn't matter that much to me. My turn will come around again. It's just that Nathan wants it so badly."

"But you are worried that people will think you were afraid because you're a girl, right?"

Lisette smiled. "You know me better than I thought! Yes, there's that."

Sergei shrugged. "Poor men, we are always at the mercy of our egos! If you were asking my advice, I would say do it. It will make you feel good, and Nathan will never find out from me."

Lisette moved her bishop recklessly.

"You mean that?"

Sergei turned an invisible key in front of his mouth.

"My lips are sealed. Now take your bishop back and try again. I'm going to win this game, but not that easily!"

Noemi was alone in the roomette. She checked the water meter and smacked it in frustration.

"Stupid thing! You're inefficient! Why can't some-one invent a better closed recovery system?"

She was depressed, she was bored, she had just had another horrible day in the kitchen. She wanted to go home; she knew she couldn't go home. She wanted a hot bath. Tears slid down her face so often now, she didn't notice them; if she shook her head, they just floated around the room.

"Stupid!" she said again, watching the tears float as little globules toward the air vent. She sat at the PC with a sudden idea.

But the system was busy, as usual. Noemi pounded the keyboard in frustration.

Ridiculous! she thought. The average human requires two quarts of water a day. We either drink it directly or get it through the food we eat and most of it, in spite of what everyone thinks, is excreted through the lungs and the skin. We exhale and perspire more water vapor than we lose through — other means.

Noemi shuddered delicately. The human body was such a gross, filthy thing, if you thought about it that way. But a truly efficient water recovery system would not only recycle waste water from cooking and showers and toilets, it would pull the water vapor out of the air as well, recycling it as usable water.

But the technology used aboard the Mars ships couldn't do that yet, and even the water recycler was less than sixty percent efficient. That was why they'd had to bring huge tanks of supplementary water aboard, taking up valuable space. And that was why everyone was down on Noemi for using too much water.

Ridiculous! Noemi thought again. Depressed and frustrated, she decided to take another shower.

"*Shalom*, Ari," Dr. Al-Wahab would say, using the Hebrew greeting whenever he and Dr. Berger met in the corridors or the commissary. "After you!"

"*Salaam*, Ali," Dr. Berger would reply in Arabic. Each man used the other one's language, as a courtesy and as a kind of in joke. "No, after you; I insist!"

The Egyptian engineer and the Israeli agronomist had trained together, roomed together, knew each other for years. The similarity of "Ali" and "Ari" got the computer confused, and they frequently got each other's messages, but it just added to the fun. And at least once a day they would meet in the commissary doorway going through this politeness routine, while the trainees enjoyed the show.

"Now, there's an example," Alice said, "of how adults can overcome differences that have been going on for generations. Pity some of us can't learn from that."

"How's that?" Ian asked, sipping noisily on his morning tea.

Alice looked at him as if she hoped he was kidding.

"Are you serious? An Arab and an Israeli getting along with each other? Think about it. And they both lost relatives in the war too."

"Which war was that?" Ian asked innocently.

Alice sighed in exasperation. "Pick one. There was one in 1948, one in 1953, another in '67 and in '73."

"Ancient history!" was Ian's opinion as he helped himself to his fourth granola bar.

"This is from someone who's still brooding over something that happened in 1916!" Alice punched him on the arm.

"Oh, no!" Ian corrected her. "Bloody Sunday was just a recent thing. We've been fighting the British in Ireland for eight hundred years."

"And look where it's got you," Alice remarked. "There's a world outside of Ireland, Ian McShane. There's even a world outside of Earth, and we're it."

"And you ought to run for president!" Ian teased her, tugging one of her braids before he shoved off. For once he was going to be on time.

Alice picked at her dinner, no longer hungry. They'd all been hungry during the first weeks of the voyage. Dr. Allen said that was normal, and encouraged them to eat frequent, small meals, as many as four or five a day, to keep their energy levels up. Now Alice found she had no appetite most of the time. She was tired of being around people all the time, tired of their bickering. All she wanted to do was stay in the lab and talk to her plants. At least they didn't talk back.

"Did I miss him?" Lanie sidled over with her dinner tray.

"Who?" Alice asked, coming out of her fog.

"Who else?" Lanie said, suddenly shy, and Alice remembered she was developing a crush on Ian.

"Yes, you missed him!" Alice snapped. "He's decided to be on time for his shift for once. And don't ask me to talk to him for you, because I won't!"

"Hey, I'm supposed to be the grouch around here!" Lanie opened the pop top on her spaghetti and meatballs; the inside was extremely hot, and

72

she burned her fingers. She wanted to curse at the thing but didn't because Alice was there. "What's wrong with you?"

"Nothing. Everything." Alice scratched her head. With Noemi using so much water, she had tried to compensate by not washing her hair as much. "I'm tired of being with people. I'm not used to crowds and I'm sick of the bickering!"

"Maybe you're the one who needs the shrink," Lanie suggested. Alice stopped scratching her head and scowled "Look, don't bite my head off; it was just an idea."

"Maybe you're right," Alice sighed. Out of the corner of her eye she could see Tara getting her breakfast, and knew she'd be heading over their way in spite of Lanie, because she wanted to talk to Alice. Well, Alice didn't want to talk to anybody. She wasn't going to hang around.

"I have to go," she told Lanie, just as Tara floated over. " 'Morning, Tara. *E noho raa.*"

"*Haare raa,*" Tara answered, frowning at Alice's sudden exit.

"Secret codes?" Lanie asked innocently. Tara would have to decide whether to be polite and stay, or be her usual rude self and stalk off.

"Alice has been teaching me some Maori phrases," Tara said, deciding to stay, though she clearly wasn't happy about it. "*E noho raa* means 'stay well.' *Haare raa* means 'go well.' Nothing secret about it."

"That's great," Lanie said sincerely, digging into

73

her dinner, which had finally cooled off. "I'm lucky if I can handle English most of the time. My teachers were always down on me for bad grammar."

"There are over forty-seven languages spoken on this ship," Tara said, sniffing suspiciously at her scrambled eggs, which were grayer than usual this morning. "However, English is still the common tongue."

"Even with all the different accents," Lanie agreed. Was it possible she and Tara were actually getting along for once? "I like Ian's accent. Jhong's is sort of cool too."

Tara decided to take a chance on the eggs after all, though she closed her eyes as she took the first bite. "Ugh!" she shuddered. "Is that why you have such a negative attitude? Your teachers being 'down on you,' I mean?"

Lanie scooped the last few strands of spaghetti out of the container before she exploded.

"What attitude?" she shouted. "You're the one who's been dishing attitude. Can I tell you something? No, wait a minute: don't interrupt me. I grew up in the projects—you know what projects are?"

"Yeah," Tara admitted. The angrier Lanie got, the cooler she was. "So?"

"It's a bunch of big, cold concrete apartment houses all clumped together," Lanie explained. "Ugly and covered with graffiti, and not a blade of grass anywhere. And all kinds of people live there. All

74

races, all colors, all religions, but we all have one thing in common — we're all poor, and we're all desperate to get out. So we learn to survive, and we learn to help each other, 'cause if even one of us gets out, it's a win for everybody, you dig? So quit treating me like I'm some spoiled cheerleader, okay?"

"I don't have to listen to this junk," Tara said calmly, watching Lanie's face turn red. "Get real."

She didn't give Lanie a chance to say anything, just floated off with her breakfast tray so that Lanie would have to shout and make a complete jerk of herself to finish the argument.

Instead, Lanie flung her empty tray at the nearby disposal shute. It frisbied out of her hand and hit the Plexiglas divider, splattering spaghetti sauce. She still ended up looking like a jerk.

I'll get you for this, Tara White; I swear I will! Lanie fumed.

"Nathan Long," the intercom boomed in Dr. Allen's crisp British accent. "Nathan Long, please report to Engineering Airlock A immediately. Nathan Long, please report —"

"What the — ?"

Nathan jerked upright in his sleep-sack so hard he bumped his head on the bulkhead. It was his offshift, and he'd been reading in his quarters. Report to the engineering airlocks? What was this all

75

about?

He slid into his clothes and hand-over-handed to engineering to find Dr. Al-Wahab standing by the airlock holding a hardsuit. Sergei was already suited up and waiting by the airlock.

"What—?" was all Nathan managed to say.

"You're going E.V.A.," Dr. Al-Wahab said as if it were no big deal. "You've got two hours of oxygen to do a one-hour job. Come on, suit up!"

Chapter Six

"Let me get this straight . . ." Nathan's voice over the helmet headset was scratchy with static. "My name was next after Lanie's on the E.V.A. roster?"

Lisette was on communications. "What's so unusual about that?" she said into her transmitter, not exactly answering the question.

"Nothing, I guess." Nathan sounded skeptical.

Dangling from his tether at the aft end of the *Santa Maria*'s hull, Sergei looked like a little puppet from where Nathan floated near the ship's midsection. The glare reflected from the hull was so strong it had polarized Sergei's helmet visor, making him invisible inside it. Nathan guessed he must look the same to Sergei. He heard the Russian boy clear his throat.

"I don't mean to interrupt this little party," he said sarcastically. "But we have less forty-three minutes left to do our job."

"Roger!" Nathan answered.

For the next several minutes, all Lisette could hear from inside the ship was both boys breathing as they covered as much of the exterior as they could, propelling themselves by the handhold rails set at intervals along the *Santa Maria's* hull, checking for flaws or damage. From time to time a white-suited figure, starkly lit against the backdrop of space, would drift past one of the E.V.A. cameras, which were recording everything to transmit back to Earth.

"Do you think he believed me?" Lisette asked Gen, keeping her hand over her own transmitter so the two boys outside the *Santa Maria* wouldn't hear. "About—about Lanie's backing out, I mean."

Gen shrugged, knowing that wasn't what she meant. "I can understand where Lanie's coming from. It's you I wonder about."

Lisette looked embarrassed. "You know?"

"I saw the roster too. Before you had Dr. Al-Wahab change it."

"You think it was stupid of me?"

"Love makes people do strange things," Gen suggested. "At least, that's what the songs say. Hey, have you got a rubber band?"

He was holding his shoulder-length hair at the back of his neck. Lisette laughed, glad he'd changed the subject.

"No, but I can braid it for you."

"It won't stay," Gen told her. "I was thinking of shaving my head."

"To go with your mustache?" Lisette teased. Gen

had spent a whole week looking like he had dirt on his upper lip before he gave up on the idea.

"Can I help it if I have to shave only once a week?"

Outside, Sergei had to keep reminding Nathan to keep his eyes on the ship, not on the stars.

"Beware of romance, my friend," he warned. "It's strictly for sloppy earthbound novels. Four hundred pages of whining, then a double suicide at the end. Keep your eyes on your work. Stargaze later."

"From here it looks as if you could reach out and grab a handful of them!" Nathan said in awe, extending one gloved hand as if to do exactly that, though he did remember to hold tight to the handrail. "You're a total pragmatist, Sergei."

"Thank you," the Russian boy said, his eyes on nothing more than the monotonous metal hull beneath his hands. They still had to check the solar wings and the navcon before they could go inside.

WELCOME TO MIDPOINT! read the banner Karl and Gen were hanging in the rec room under Nathan's supervision. Below them, Ian finished neutralizing his last enemy space alien and whooped in triumph.

"High score, high score!" he yelled, entering his

initials and doing backflips until he crashed into Gen. They traded high-fives while Karl looked on disapprovingly.

"This is a person who daily has a Blaster under his hand!" He shook his head. "It worries me."

"What's he going to do?" Gen wondered, grabbing the banner again. "Here, hold your end up a little more while I stick this on, will you? There's nobody out here but our three ships. Is he going to start a revolution?"

"That's what worries me!" Karl said darkly.

It had been exactly one hundred and five days since they'd left Icarus, and they were right on schedule. Within the next five days they would reach the exact midpoint of their journey and make the final course corrections that would put them in the path of Mars. The *Nina* and *Pinta* were also on schedule, and near enough so that there was no noticeable time lag in radio transmissions. Of course, the time lag with Earth was getting longer the farther they traveled.

The midpoint party had been Nathan's idea, with Dr. Allen's approval. She had decided the crew needed something to take their minds off their petty grievances, the boredom of the everyday routine, and the fact that there were still one hundred and ten days to go.

The party would happen in five days, on the one hundred and tenth day out, and would overlap both shifts. Everyone who wasn't needed at a duty station would be there. Even those on duty could keep the intercoms open at least. The idea spread to the *Nina* and *Pinta;* it was going to be one big interplanetary good time.

"Will you play for us?" Karl asked Gen as they finally got the banner straight.

The rocker looked uneasy. "I wasn't planning to. I'm so out of practice! What about you? You still practice about an hour every day; I've heard you. I'll play if you will."

"I don't think the rest of the crew shares my taste in music," Karl said.

It was true. While Karl could listen to rock with the best of them, his heart really belonged in the eighteenth century, with Haydn and Mozart and Beethoven. He'd brought an electronic keyboard along, and practiced methodically for at least an hour a day. He was good enough to practice his fingering without even turning the keyboard on, so he didn't end up disturbing the neighbors the way Gen did.

"But it's not the same as a piano," he said sadly. "Of all the things from Earth, I shall miss the piano the most."

As a substitute, he'd begun hanging out in the hydroponics lab whenever he was offshift, not because he had any great fondness for plants, but because of Dr. Berger's music tapes. Karl and the agronomist spent hours talking about classical music; Dr. Berger respected Karl's opinions on the subject as much as he would an adult's.

"Metallica?" Ian would shout whenever he and Gen got together, especially if Gen was wearing his Metallica T-shirt. "Get out! Not a bit of it. U2, for my money!"

"U2 isn't heavy metal," Gen would say, undisturbed.

"There's more to life than heavy metal," Ian would argue.

"White Snake," Gen would say with a grin, and Ian would pretend to be furious.

"You call yourself a rocker?" he would bellow. "You're daft. Van Halen!"

"Sugarcubes."

"Never heard of 'em."

"You call yourself a rocker?" Gen would throw Ian's words right back at him. "They're only the hottest thing out of Iceland . . ."

They did it whenever they were together—bellowed and insulted each other, sang snatches of favorite songs or played air guitar riffs to drown each other out. It was as if there were some secret code between them.

"How'd Genshiro ever get on the same team as a stiff like you?" Ian goaded Karl whenever they crossed paths.

Karl ignored him, practicing his keyboard fingering the way Gen played his air guitar. Ian got tired of harassing someone who wouldn't fight back, and Karl would study him out of the corner of his eye. Dr. Allen had chewed him out about the hardware; he no longer wore the bikers' boots, though he kept the gloves. The heavy gold chain around his neck had disappeared, and the oversize crucifix now dangled from a gold ring in his left ear.

He still wore his coveralls with the sleeves ripped out to show off his tattoo, or else he rolled his T-shirt sleeves for the same reason.

I suppose he thinks the girls like that! Karl thought, disgusted.

It so happened one of them did. Lanie started hanging around the flying bridge on her offshift.

"Hey, neat tag," she'd said the first time Ian flexed his biceps and she noticed the tattoo. "Where'd you get it?"

"My brother did it for me," Ian said with a catch in his voice. "My brother Rob that was shot."

"Oh, I'm sorry!" Lanie said, all sympathetic.

Which is exactly what Ian was counting on! Karl brooded, watching the two of them fawning all over each other. What was the English expression about birds of a feather? It looked as if juvenile delinquents also flocked together.

It was no surprise when Ian and Lanie showed

up at the midpoint party holding hands.

" 'Another one bites the dust . . .' " Gen crooned.

Karl scowled at him.

"It's all well and good for you to joke!" he said. "But she spends too much time hanging about when we are working!"

"Gives you claustrophobia, does she? Come on, Karl, chill out!" Gen slapped his shoulder playfully. "Tell you what: I'll play 'In-a-Gadda-da-Vida' during my second set if you'll do the organ solo."

Karl's eyes widened. "What will we do for percussion? You can't fake Iron Butterfly on a synthesizer."

"Leave that to me!" Gen said mysteriously. "Just let me borrow your keyboard for about an hour."

The Plexiglas partitions separating the three sections of the rec room were pulled back. The gym equipment and the ergobike were put away, the kitchen area was kept busy heating up refreshments and popping popcorn. Ian and Lanie disappeared for a while, with Ian muttering something about "bloody industrial-strength lighting," and suddenly every light in the rec room dimmed. For a second there was near panic.

"What happened?"

"A power failure?"

"Can't be. Everything else is working."

Ian quickly reappeared.

"Not to worry, folks. Just trying to give it a romantic mood. Wish I could give you disco lights, but this is the best I can do."

"Incoming for you, Chuvakin." Lisette was stuck minding communications and wasn't in the best of moods. She caught Sergei on his way to his room to spruce up for the party.

Sergei expected her to hand him a hard-copy printout of the radio message. Instead, Lisette handed him her headset. He put it on.

"Sergei Mikhailovitch?" It was Ludmilla, calling in from the *Nina*. Sergei's heart sank into his Velcro-heeled slippers.

"Ludmilla Semyonovna," he replied formally. He was not going to be lured into some sticky romantic conversation. Not when he was on his way to a party. Not with the possibility of a dozen of Ludmilla's friends listening in on the other end. "You are well?"

"I miss you," Ludmilla replied. "Since we are both attending a party tonight, I was thinking how much better it would be if we could be together."

"We will have all the time in the world to be together on Mars," Sergei said, shuddering at the thought.

"I cannot stay on the radio long," Ludmilla said.

"But I wanted you to know I will be thinking of you all night."

"That's — good, Ludmilla Semyonovna," Sergei said, knowing what she was going to ask him next.

"And will you also be thinking of me?"

"All night. I promise."

"Raisa Feodorovna also sends her regards," Ludmilla said.

I'll just bet she does! Sergei thought. He could see the two of them, talking behind their hands and giggling about him.

"Please send her my regards as well," he replied.

"I will," Ludmilla promised. "Good night, Sergei Mikhailovitch."

"Good night, Ludmilla."

"Man, what a scruffy-looking bunch!" Lanie remarked, looking around the rec room and shaking her head.

Even in the dim light Ian had provided, the others could see she was right. Most of the girls had tried to use the little makeup they had left. Those who had tans had maintained them under the ultraviolet lamps in the gym, but they were all wearing the same clothes, no matter how personalized with sewn-on patches, and their hair was a universal disaster.

Hairspray was banned in a recycled atmosphere,

and even mousse and gel were not a good idea; they built up in the drains and made them less efficient. Worse, high-pressure showers and Mission Control-issue shampoo just didn't cut it. And except for Tara's natural close curls and Lanie's boyish crop, most people were in serious need of a trim.

Lanie, of course, could afford to be smug, with Ian hanging on her arm.

"I think you look spiffy!" he whispered in her ear. His own hair was naturally spiky, shaved on the sides and standing upright on top. "Me and Sieggie, with his military crop, are the only boys who look neat. And you're the best looking of the girls."

"Don't make fun of Karl," Lanie said. "Stop calling him Sieggie."

"Why?" Ian whispered. "I thought you couldn't stand him either."

"I can't," Lanie admitted. "But he's one of my team, so I have to defend him."

"I hear Dr. Allen is going to lecture us about water use again," Karl announced, knowing Lanie and Ian were talking about him even if he couldn't hear what they were saying. "We shall all have to take fewer showers, you'll see."

He was being his usual stiff self, even at a party. A kind of uncomfortable silence settled around him, as if no one knew what to say next.

Dr. Allen never got a chance to give her lecture. Gen showed up with his guitar, and proceeded to plug in and tune it. "Come on, everybody, let's rock!"

When the music got cranked up, so did the audience. But they soon realized that Mission Control forgot to train them for dancing in zero G. Kids were bumping into everything, doing weird flips all over The Commons. Even Gen had to duck when Nathan went flying past.

Alice and Tara had had to drag Noemi to the party, and only the fear of making her eye liner run had prevented her from bursting into tears.

"I look awful!" she had cried, staring in disbelief at the reflection in her mirror.

"In your dreams!" Lisette said sarcastically before she had to leave for her comm shift.

"No, but look—I have no nails left, my complexion has gone sallow, and my hair—!"

"We all look awful," Alice said, looking glumly at the split ends on her braids, offering Noemi no sympathy. "You sit here and sulk, and I'm reporting you to Dr. Allen. Now, come on!"

She'd allowed them to drag her to the party for a while. But none of the boys paid any attention to her; she wasn't used to that. When the dancing started, she quietly slipped out.

"Where's Noemi?" Dr. Allen asked. "I wanted to ask her to do a theoretical model on the asteroid belt before we got too far into it."

No one had seen Noemi for a while.

"No big deal!" Lanie said, too loud as usual. "I know exactly where she is. In quarters again, taking another shower!"

"Does she do that often?" Dr. Allen asked, suddenly curious.

"Whenever she's depressed," Tara answered. "Which is most of the time."

"Yeah!" Lanie added, realizing she and Tara were in agreement. "I'd like to find the hot water shut-off valve and teach her a lesson."

"Me too!" Tara said, a dangerous gleam in her eye.

It was like magic. The two girls practically flew down the corridors.

"Dr. Allen!" Alice cried in horror. "You can't let them do that!"

"It's not my responsibility," Dr. Allen said. "You people are to learn to govern yourselves, and you've done admirably so far. They won't hurt Noemi."

"I don't *think* so," Alice said, not sure.

"*Has* she been using more than her quota of water?" Dr. Allen wanted to know.

Alice nodded. "Ever since we left. The rest of us have been using less so the computers wouldn't notice."

"There you are!" Dr. Allen said. "Once on Mars, there will be life-and-death decisions to be made, not something as trivial as hair. There is no place for selfishness in this colony, and the sooner Noemi learns that, the better."

"Still . . ." Alice launched herself off the nearest bulkhead. "I'd better go back there and make sure no one gets hurt."

Chapter Seven

"She isn't very strong," Lanie huffed, out of breath. "She barely passed the physicals. You want to hold the shower shut while I work the valve."

"I don't know," Tara huffed beside her. "Maybe we should give her the choice. Either she gets out of the shower, or we freeze her out. I don't want to hurt her."

"Give Noemi a choice and she'll just cry and work on your sympathies," Lanie warned.

"Doesn't matter," Tara said. "I can be tough."

"Yeah," Lanie said. They had almost reached their roomette. "I'll bet you had to be where you grew up. Just like I did."

They reached the doorway and stopped to catch their breath, hooking themselves to the Velcro wall panels to collect their nerve.

"I'm sorry I've been so hard on you," Tara said. "But living in New York City kind of makes you mean, you know?" The faraway look in her eyes told Lanie just how bad it had been. "I got into the habit of hitting first, before anyone could hit on me."

"You never hit on Alice," Lanie pointed out, more than a little jealous.

"Alice is different," Tara pointed out. "She grew up on a farm and is kind of easy-going. But you came on so tough, I thought—"

"I guess I did," Lanie admitted.

"Guess we both have to learn when to back off," Tara suggested.

"Yeah," Lanie said. They both slapped high-fives.

They expected to find Noemi in the shower, and planned to jump her as soon as she came out. To their surprise, she was working at the PC.

She didn't bother to look up when they floated in on either side of her. Noemi kept tapping a series of equations into the PC; a weird-looking graphic began to form on the screen.

"Are you satisfied?" she demanded of Lanie, turning away from the PC to glare at Tara, too. "Two against one?"

"No one's ganging up on you, Noemi." Alice rushed in, expecting to find a hair-pulling match, not this peaceful scene. "We're just reminding you that we're a team."

Noemi's eyes were red-rimmed. Her lower lip trembled as she studied the graphic on the PC screen.

"I guess I forgot that for a while," she admitted. "Maybe this will make up for things."

She pressed PRINT and sat with her hands in

her lap. There were printers in engineering, in communications, and in the rec room. Soon everyone on the ship would see the hard copy of Noemi's idea.

Her three roommates put their three very different heads together and studied the graphic on the monitor.

"It's a theoretical model to improve water recovery in a closed-cycle system," Noemi explained.

"We knew that!" Lanie said, relieved that Noemi had explained it anyway.

The PC's cursor signaled DOCUMENT PRINTED. Noemi cleared the screen and began tapping in sequences of numbers.

"Closed-system water recycling was first demonstrated under laboratory conditions in 1959," she explained, her eyes on the monitor. "The system we have does work, but it's inefficient. It recycles only actual waste water—from the showers and toilets, and from cooking runoff. And a big percentage of it is lost in the process.

"If we improved the recapture on waste water," she went on, showing her listeners the numbers on the screen, "and if we upgraded the system to recapture the water vapor in the air, which we excrete through breathing and perspiration—"

"So?" Lanie said impatiently.

"*So*," Tara said, catching on, "if we reclaim the water vapor from the air-filtration system—"

"We'll have a recyling system that's *twice* as efficient," Noemi finished, recalling the model on the screen. "See?"

She sat back and let the other three admire her work. Applied mathematics bored her, but sometimes it was necessary to show off a little. Noemi was amazed at how good she felt, for the first time since they'd left Icarus.

"You're a genius!" Alice announced, hugging her.

Soon all four girls were hugging and giggling, sharing the triumph. Lanie and Tara hugged last.

"Took us long enough!" Lanie said. If she didn't mouth off, she was afraid she'd go all mushy.

"I'll remind you that the trouble started with you—" Tara began, but Alice shushed them both.

"That's enough, both of you! Let's get back to the party before Gen starts to play again."

Gen hadn't told anyone but his "tech crew" what he had planned for the second set. He and Sergei and Ian had spent hours reprogramming the percussion on Karl's keyboard to come up with the closest thing to Iron Butterfly's exotic rhythms. Karl looked on, wringing his hands and worrying.

"It's the bass I'm worried about," Gen said. " 'In-A-Gadda-Da-Vida's' percussion you can imitate, but it's those weird elephant sounds Lee Dorman used to lay down in the piece. How're you going to mimic those?"

"Look, there's your bass," Ian said, showing him.

94

Karl looked over his shoulder and nodded. "All you've got to do is key it in sequence. Karl's gonna have to remember where everything goes, including the drum solo before his organ overlay. It's all by the numbers."

"I can do it," Karl said, not all that sure himself.

"If you say so," Gen said. They couldn't even practice together without someone overhearing and giving away the surprise.

Now Ian had gone off to fool with the lights some more, and Karl set up his keyboard close to Gen.

"I'm really nervous," he confided now that Ian was out of earshot. "The organ is the whole piece here."

"You'll be fine," Gen said confidently, tuning up.

Ian came back. "Strobes," he reported. "Interfaced, so they should key in to what you're playing. But I wish I could really tinker. I'd give you disco lights and everything."

"Maybe next time," Gen said, a little wary of too much gimmickry taking away from his music. "Nathan wants to do another one of these when we get through the asteroids. There's time."

On Ian's prearranged signal, the lights went down completely, then came up with a single spot on Karl. Swallowing nervously, the German boy took a deep breath, touched his fingers to the keyboard, and played the opening notes of Iron Butterfly's "In-a-Gadda-da-Vida."

95

Iron Butterfly was an old band, classic heavy metal from the sixties. "In-a-Gadda-da-Vida" was an old song, made before anyone here except the supervisors had been born. But almost every serious rock fan knew it, and there was a cheer of recognition for the opening chords. And when Ian's strobe lights began to pulse in time to the music, the crowd went wild.

On the flying bridge Dr. Al-Wahab finished his systems check. The intercom brought him the music from the rec room, and he shook his head.

"Remarkable!" he said quietly to himself, drumming his fingers in time to the music.

In the hydroponics lab Dr. Berger shut off the Mozart tape and opened the intercom to let his plants hear Iron Butterfly as well.

"Better get used to it, children," he told them.

Alone on capcom Lisette was also listening to the music. She tried not to feel sorry for herself for missing the party. Suddenly someone crept up behind her and covered her eyes with his hands.

Lisette gasped and pulled the fingers away, knowing who it was.

"Nathan!"

"Couldn't leave my best girl all alone up here," he said. "How're things?"

"Oh, a laugh a minute!" she said glumly. "I just finished talking to a dear friend of yours."

Nathan gave her a puzzled look. "Who?"

"Suki. She said to tell you she and Dr. Thompson have worked out a trajectory that'll cut three days off their travel time so *Nina* will get to Mars ahead of us."

Typical Suki, Nathan thought. Not too long ago her competitiveness would have made him furious. Not anymore.

"Who cares?" he said as the music from the rec room filled the space around them. Karl was laying his beautiful organ tones over the preprogrammed drum solo. "When will Suki learn that first isn't always best?"

"You're right about one thing," Lisette sighed, draping the headset around her neck and leaning against his shoulder.

"What's that?" Nathan murmured. Her hair was tickling his nose.

"Who cares?" Lisette said.

A lot of things felt better after the midpoint party. It wasn't as if anything changed though. The living arrangements were just as crowded, and the lack of privacy was just as nerve-racking as before. The prepackaged meals were just as boring. The work shifts had become so routine, most people could do their jobs in their sleep. The mandatory two hours of exercise daily was just as grueling. But somehow people's moods improved.

Maybe it was realizing that their journey was half over. Once they reached the actual midpoint of their journey, the midcourse correction maneuvers meant they would lose communication with Earth and with their sister ships for several days, until the Canopus lock was reestablished. That was scary until Dr. Al-Wahab explained it.

"The star Canopus is the second brightest star in our sky," the ship's engineer explained. "We use it and the sun to triangulate and give us accurate navigation. If you can imagine the *Santa Maria* as being hung from a long cord hanging in space, it will spin and lose direction if we don't "lock" it onto something stationary and easy to find. That's Canopus."

The pioneers had all had at least a basic astrophysics course. They understood this much.

"Now, when we make midcourse corrections, we will lose the Canopus lock temporarily. We will experience a communications blackout, but our computer tracking will get us back on course, and that will be the true midpoint of our journey."

The midcourse corrections had gone without a hitch, and while it was scary being out in space with no one to talk to, once it was over everyone relaxed. And on Day 110 there was to be a special broadcast from Earth. The secretary general of the United Nations, along with leaders of many of the nations who had pioneers aboard, would speak to them on Earth-wide television. Halfway to Mars, they would be the biggest news on Earth.

Meanwhile, life went on with a few changes. The bull sessions in The Commons still went on for hours, but they were different. People actually listened to one another instead of always shouting each other down. The Spaceball tournament was now a round-the-clock event, with team standings posted on the computer net daily. People laughed more. They spent less time missing what they'd left behind on Earth and more time planning for the adventure of Mars.

With Lanie's help on the computer, Dr. Al-Wahab was able to put Noemi's improved water recycling system into practice. Dr. Al-Wahab filed a report with Mission Control, and soon the *Nina* and the *Pinta* were upgrading their recovery systems as well. Noemi was the hero of the day.

"I'd love to hear what Suki Long had to say about that!" Nathan said.

"The important thing," Dr. Al-Wahab reminded them, "is that hereafter this model can be used to improve closed-cycle recovery systems on all future Mars vessels. It's a great breakthrough."

"The important thing," Sergei teased, tugging one of Noemi's curls, "is that Noemi gets to take more showers!"

Instead of going into a sulk, Noemi laughed along with her friends.

Gen's troubles were over too. Some of the engineering crew cleared a space in the cargo hold, where he could practice his guitar. Sometimes Karl would bring his keyboard and they would practice together or, when Karl was in a "classical" mood, separately. As word got around, other crew members started to show up. Some played various instruments; some came to listen. The cargo hold became the place for a round-the-clock jam session.

Radio station SNAP continued to flourish. An astrobatics team was forming, and Sergei's chess club added a few new members. There were even plans to start a theater group.

Some things didn't change. Ian developed a grudging respect for Karl's talents as a musician, but he and the German boy still didn't get along. They were the best of the copilot team, but only one of them could be Dr. Allen's copilot when they were ready to soft-land on Mars. Their rivalry was intense. And Lanie was still hanging out with Ian, which made Karl furious.

"Lanie's asked me not to call you Sieggie anymore," Ian said when they were running their daily systems check. "I'm doing it only because of her."

"How magnanimous of you!" Karl sneered. "Perhaps now that you already have a girl, you can roll down your sleeves and stop showing off that ugly tattoo!"

Ian made a fist, then remembered where he was.

"Delicate equipment," he remarked. "If this was the Belfast streets, boyo, I'd punch your lights out."

"I doubt it," Karl said dangerously. "I placed third

in kick-boxing in my secondary school."

"Only third?" Ian asked. "And I thought you were perfect! Suppose I asked you to prove that?"

"Name the day!" was all Karl said.

Then there were the things that got worse.

"Sanjay and I have been keeping a record," Alice reported to Dr. Allen. Sanjay was from the New Delhi program and a qualified paramedic, as Alice was. "Between us we've treated over thirty assorted gashes and abrasions within the last month, some serious enough to require stitches."

"That's fairly high," Dr. Allen remarked. "What's causing it?"

"Dropped tools, misjudging distances at point three eight G when we're more used to zero," Alice said. "What's worrying us, though, is the broken bones."

Dr. Allen frowned. She'd set only one broken wrist since they'd left Icarus.

"Bones, plural? Why wasn't I informed?"

"It's mostly fingers or toes, and they'd rather Sanjay or I set them. Most people are too embarrassed to bother you about it." Alice handed Dr. Allen a clipboard where she'd been keeping track. "Eleven fingers and five toes, all within the past two weeks. Not all of them seem to be impact related. For a while that was getting to be a joke. Someone was always yelling 'Heads up!' just as something came flying, *spang*, right past you. But Sanjay and I think some of these may be pressure breaks. Calcium related."

Dr. Allen turned on the PC in her tiny infirmary and waited for it to come online.

"Any other symptoms?" she asked. "Nausea, abdominal pain, frequent urination? Things they'd complain about without necessarily seeing me?"

Alice shook her head. "Not that I've heard. Just too many broken bones."

The computer signaled READY and Dr. Allen called up the file she wanted.

"This is why we've asked all of you for a blood sample every thirty days."

Alice nodded. Everyone complained about the finger-sticking she and Sanjay had to do, and she'd had an awful time of it at first, trying to keep the blood in the tiny pipette instead of bouncing in little globules all over the infirmary.

"Okay," Dr. Allen said. "This indicates mild hypercalcemia in a few people, notably the ones who hate to exercise. Once we showed them the rise in their calcium levels, they were back in the gym immediately. This was last month's file. The last blood tests were completed yesterday. Let's see what the new results are."

The file came up, listing each crew member's name and current blood calcium level. A normal blood calcium reading should be between 8.8 and 10.4 milligrams per one hundred milliliters of blood. Any more calcium than that in the blood-stream meant it was leaching out of the bones, and that was dangerous. Short-term, it meant increased brittleness of the long bones and a greater chance of pressure breaks. Untreated, hypercalcemia could be fatal.

"Fewer than a half dozen are borderline." Dr. Allen showed Alice the readings. "People have different metabolic rates. I'll go after these few with calcium supplements."

She shut off the PC.

"The rest just has to be clumsiness. Remember that we're all experiencing a one to two percent bone density loss for every month we spend in zero G. It's normal and there's nothing to be done about it, and it's why we can't return to Earth. But you lab workers should be adapting more readily to point three eight G than the rest of us, and that should make it easier for you to adapt once we land on Mars. If you don't kill each other with flying garden tools first."

"Dr. Berger has warning signs posted all over," Alice said. " 'Put Tools in Their Place,' 'Know Where Your Crewmates Are.' It doesn't seem to help. Maybe if you gave them a pep talk . . ."

"It's going to take something more radical than that," Dr. Allen said.

What it took was Nathan ending up with his ankle in a cast.

"Of all the stupid stunts!" Dr. Allen said as Sanjay and Alice helped her strap Nathan to the folddown infirmary table so she could set his broken ankle. "This isn't like you at all, Nathan! What were you thinking of?"

Nathan grimaced in pain. He didn't think anything could hurt this bad. It was almost as if he could hear the broken ends of the bones grinding together inside his leg.

"I thought I had my timing down!" was all he said.

"Well, you obviously didn't!" Dr. Allen snapped. "I won't waste the lidocaine on you; we have only so much. You're going to have to be a hero while I set this without anesthesia.

"Out!" she yelled at everyone crowding the infirmary door. News traveled fast.

"Nathan Long fell off his skateboard and broke his ankle!"

"What was he doing on a skateboard in zero G?"

"Trying to go over the top of the hydroponics wheel!"

The hydroponics lab rotated along an ingeniously housed track mechanism that allowed just enough room for people to pass on all sides of its arc except where it was attached to the track housing. Nathan had been studying the clearance on these passageways, and the speed of the lab's rotation, for weeks.

"You're out of your mind, mate!" Ian said when

Nathan told him what he was planning.

"Totally!" Lanie agreed.

"I don't want to know about it," Gen said, heading off to practice. Karl wasn't around, or he'd have been sure to have something to say against it.

"You will fall on your butt, and Suki Long will never let you forget it once she hears." Sergei grinned. "May I watch?"

"No problem," Nathan said coolly, shifting his skateboard out from under his arm. "I'm in complete control."

The key to the maneuver was to stay on the crest of the wave and jump off before you got anywhere near the rotation mechanism. Nathan walked the outer rim of the wheel several times, then took a few practice runs along the lower half of the curve to get used to gravity again after all this time, jumping off before he reached the zenith and trying again. He wasn't about to be reckless, not with all these people watching. It was amazing how fast the news traveled, and there was already quite a crowd.

Once he got the maneuver down, Nathan should have been able to skate around the entire outer rim of the lab, his momentum creating its own gravity so that the skateboard's wheels stayed on the rim. He planned to go over the top and jump off, tipping the board up into his hand just before he got too near the rotation mechanism.

Except he hadn't calculated on the racket his skate wheels would make, so loud they could be

105

heard inside the lab, which meant Dr. Berger had to come out to investigate. It was the sight of his scowling face with its bright red beard that freaked Nathan enough to lose his footing. He grabbed the board as he fell. All he remembered after that was pain.

"Idiotic, Mr. Long!" Dr. Al-Wahab said when he found out. Alice and Sanjay were on the scene, examining Nathan to find out that his ankle was broken. "You might have damaged the rotation mechanism. Perhaps severely enough to halt the rotation. And then what?"

"I had it timed—" Nathan began before the pain in his ankle made him gasp.

Dr. Al-Wahab shook his head. "There will have to be a general briefing about this. I never would have expected you to do anything so irresponsible."

Irresponsible, Nathan thought, bracing himself as Dr. Allen grasped his foot and his leg just above the break, preparing to force the bone back into place. He gritted his teeth and tried not to scream, but some noise must have come from his throat because . . .

It was awfully sore by the time he came around. Had he actually fainted? What a wimp! When he opened his eyes, Lisette was leaning over him, fire in her eyes.

"How immature!" she accused him. "All of this for a skateboard trick! *Imbecile!*"

Nathan lay back on the infirmary table. Somehow

106

Lisette's accusation hurt worse than his ankle.

"I've given you a flexible cast," Dr. Allen told him. Her face and voice were grim. "You won't exactly be putting any pressure on it without gravity, and it may actually heal faster. Just don't bang it into anything. If you're lucky, you'll be out of the cast before we land."

"I really stepped in it this time, didn't I?" Nathan asked weakly. Was everyone on the ship mad at him?

"You could put it that way," Dr. Allen said, loosening the straps that held him to the table. "You're off the E.V.A. roster permanently. Report to The Commons right now. Dr. Berger is holding a briefing."

Chapter Eight

"If we were on Earth, this skateboard incident would be no more than a childish prank," Dr. Berger said. "Immature, certainly. Dangerous? To the boy on the skateboard, potentially so. A childish prank, to be disciplined with demerits or restriction to quarters. But put it in the context of the needs of this ship, and of this whole expedition, and it becomes something far more serious."

Nathan sat in the middle of the crowd in The Commons, trying not to squirm.

"The fact is," Dr. Berger went on, "that the rotation housing is built to withstand precisely the sort of damage the skateboard might have caused. And by now our plants are well rooted and flourishing, and more dependent upon light source than geotropism. In all probability they would survive even if the gravity failed. But it is not a risk we should have to take.

Without the plants we do not have sufficient oxygen, much less an independent food source. And without these two essentials . . ."

Dr. Berger didn't have to finish his thought. Everyone could figure it out for themselves. Nathan felt their silent accusations and hung his head. He had never felt so ashamed.

"Since there is no formal government aboard the *Santa Maria,* and since the hydroponics lab is my department, Dr. Allen has left the question of punishment up to me," Dr. Berger went on after what felt like forever. "I will not treat you like a child, Nathan Long. The humiliation you are feeling right now, and the cast around your ankle, will remain with you to remind you of what you've done. I do think it's fair, however, to forbid you to attend the United Nations ceremonies."

There was a murmur of disbelief. Some of the pioneers thought the punishment was too harsh.

"If it was up to me, I'd've tossed him E.V.A. in his underwear!" Ian whispered.

"That's exactly why it isn't up to you!" Karl snapped back. He could understand perfectly the guilt Nathan was feeling.

Nathan swallowed hard and raised his head at last.

"Yes, sir," he said slowly. "If you think that's fair, Dr. Berger, then I can deal with it."

If he had been in charge, Nathan thought, he would have locked himself up somewhere and thrown away the key. As it was, knowing that of all the team leaders he would be the only one restricted from speaking with the U.N. secretary general and the TV people would have to do. His mother would wonder, and he'd have to send her a message telling her what he'd done, so she wouldn't worry. And Suki would certainly find out and, as Sergei had said, only joking, she would never let him forget it.

Which didn't matter as much as the fact that Lisette might never speak to him again.

"You should lighten up on him," Gen told Lisette while they waited for the secretary general to get back to them on video. This far from Earth there was a time lag of several minutes between transmissions; they had to wait for the secretary general to get their message, then wait again while he sent his message back. It was nerve-racking, but there was no other way to do it.

"No way!" Lisette answered. "He acted like a jerk. Let him suffer for it!"

"Cold-hearted woman!" Gen remarked. The secretary general's face on the screen began to move again; his voice came over Gen's transmitter, and Gen made sure the intercom was open so the entire ship could hear.

". . . and in conclusion, I wish to inform these courageous youngsters that all of Earth supports what they do this historic day . . ."

"It's like watching Max Headroom," Gen cracked, grateful no one on Earth could hear him. "W-w-w-ish to in-in-in-form these c-c-c-courageous youngsters—"

"Cut it out!" Lisette said.

"Sorry!" Gen said, and burst into giggles. "Is it me, or does it suddenly seem less important what people on Earth think about us?"

"What do you mean?"

Gen waved his hand at the screen, where the secretary general was still droning on. Before him the President of the United States, the Soviet Premier, the Japanese Prime Minister, and representatives of most of the governments on Earth had had something to say; the broadcast had been going on for two hours already.

"Listen to them," Gen said. "One after the other, all telling us how proud they are of us, what a brave thing we're doing, how we're now part of history."

"What would you like them to say? That they're glad to get rid of us?"

"I don't know," Gen admitted. "But we know all that stuff. It's not important anymore. We've got a job to do, and we're doing it, period."

"It's the time lag. It doesn't seem real because of the time lag. Max Headroom, as you say."

"Or maybe we've outgrown Earth. What's important to it doesn't matter to us anymore," Gen said, and was suddenly very depressed. But, being Gen, his mood didn't last long. "Hey, know what I can't wait for? My first lobster dinner on Mars!"

"Lobster?" Lisette echoed. "Are you crazy? What lobster? We'll be living on leaves and twigs and Dr. Berger's strawberries for years."

"Guess again," Gen said. "I know something you

don't know!"

Lisette thought about that. Gen's specialty was biology. There was a special refrigerated compartment in engineering marked BIOTECH: AUTHORIZATION REQUIRED, and only Dr. Berger and the bio students knew what was in there.

"Like what?!"

"Well, I don't know," Gen teased. "What's it worth to you? Enough to stop giving Nathan the chill?"

"That's none of your business!" Lisette tossed her dark curls. "Besides, I intended only to make him suffer for a little while. Now, tell me!"

"Hold on!" Gen said, flicking toggles so Dr. Allen could answer a question put to her by one of the representatives on Earth. "Okay, first you tell me: what do lobsters, snails, and catfish all have in common?"

Lisette frowned. "Come on, you know I'm no biologist. I give up!"

"They're all bottom feeders. Scavengers. They feed on waste products in riverbeds or on the ocean floor. Including human wastes."

"Ugh!" Lisette shuddered. "You mean I've been eating *escargots* all these years, and they've been eating—I don't want to think about it!"

"Well, think about this," Gen went on. "In the BioTech fridge are several thousand fertilized eggs. Catfish, lobsters, and snails. The temperatures are very carefully controlled, and they'll keep indefinitely. But once we've established living quarters on Mars, and a waste-management system—"

"Escargots!" Lisette's eyes lit up at the thought.

"Or lobster," Gen added.

"Every night!" they said together.

"I still don't understand how you can aim for something that isn't there," Alice said.

Nathan didn't answer her at first. He couldn't help thinking she'd come to visit him at his work station only because she was feeling sorry for him.

"Didn't you pay attention to anything during astrophysics?" he asked in disbelief.

"I took only 101, and barely passed," Alice said. "I'm an agronomist, not an astrophysicist. I won't test you on tree grafting or ergot infestations if you don't make fun of what I don't know about astronomy."

Nathan sighed. "So what do you want to know?"

"I know it sounds dumb, but I sort of assumed you launched your ship from Earth, pointed it at Mars, and fired it like an arrow straight on. I don't understand about Canopus locks or triangulation, and if we're really are freefalling through space, it scares me to death."

She really was trying to make him feel better, Nathan decided. They'd studied all this stuff before. He found himself explaining anyway.

"Okay, look, this is how it goes." He called up the correct display on a nearby terminal. "Mars can be anywhere from thirty-five to two hundred fifty million miles from Earth, depending upon where each planet is in its orbit. The ideal is to pick a time for launch when they're closest and aim for Mars then.

But since we don't have the technology to fly in a straight line, and because we're not aiming at where Mars *is*, but at where it's *going to be* by the time we get there, we're actually traveling in a big arc, millions of miles farther than the actual distance."

Alice nodded. "Okay, I get that part. If Mars is *here* when we leave"—she pointed—"it'll be *there* seven months later when we arrive. But why can't we go *there* in a straight line?"

"If we could feel what Karl calls constant-thrust technology, we could. We could get to Mars in much less time according to him. But we don't, so we can't. And there's no way we can carry enough fuel to push a ship this size all the way to Mars, so what we do is use gravity wells." He called up a second display. "First Earth's, then the moon's. These push us in the right direction. Then we freefall to midpoint, where we make the necessary course corrections, then use the gravity of Mars to pull us in. We'll have to travel out of our way to get there, but it works."

"Whew! So what we're actually doing is dropping like a rock through space?" Alice shuddered. "That's horrifying!"

"Well, yeah, but we do control it by means of the Canopus lock. And because the computers know where we're supposed to be going, all we have to do is keep readjusting our actual trajectory to match the one stored in their memory banks. From here on we're actually decelerating instead of accelerating."

Alice watched him call it up on the screen.

"It's still horrifying," she said. "I don't know about

you, but I'll be grateful to have some dirt under my feet again, even if it is Mars red and not New Zealand black."

"I'll just be grateful to get this cast off my leg so everybody'll stop staring at me," Nathan said. "Not that I'm looking for sympathy or anything."

"No, of course not."

"I deserve everything I got for pulling such a lame-brained stunt."

"Yes, you do," Alice agreed. "But in case you're interested, there hasn't been one more broken bone since yours. Accidents in the lab are way, way down. So you did accomplish some good."

"You're not saying that to make me feel good?"

"Who, me?" Alice asked innocently. "I'm with Lisette. I think you were a jerk."

"Yeah," Nathan said. It was time to change the subject. "Are you really that eager to get to land again?"

Alice nodded. "I'm a farmer. Space is very nice, but it's just space. Land is where things grow. Don't tell me you're not bored with being in this big tin can?"

"Not me," Nathan said with a faraway look in his eye. "I only wish I could live long enough to where Mars is just a stepping-stone to the whole universe, and to know I've been a part of that."

"S-i-n-n-f-e-i-n." Lanie spelled out the letters in Ian's tattoo. "What's it mean?"

"Shinfine," Ian corrected her. "It means 'Ourselves Alone.' The slogan of the Irish Republican Army."

"The ones that plant bombs in restaurants and baby carriages," Lanie said, testing him. "That's one way to make sure they're 'themselves alone'!"

"They're the ones that're going to make Ireland a free nation once again, free and united!' Ian said stubbornly.

"You really believe that?" Lanie demanded. "Are you that stupid, to think blowing up innocent people is going to get you what you want?"

"Not so much anymore," Ian admitted, stretching lazily before he put his arm around her shoulder. "Funny how things change once you back up a bit and have a hard look at them. When I think I might've killed somebody, or been killed like my brother Rob—"

"—and I would never have met you!" Lanie finished for him.

"Fancy that!" Ian said.

Karl hadn't intended to eavesdrop. He'd been grabbing a quick snack in The Hub Café before reporting for his work shift. He'd spent most of his free time lately working the old-fashioned microfiche scanner in the ship's "library."

Most of the trainees and all of the adults had brought a few favorite books along, and these had been swapped back and forth until the covers were worn off. But for serious research you had to request a computer file from Earth, which might take hours or even days to come through the computer. Besides,

116

you had to give a reason for the request. Or you had to work the crank on the microfiche scanner until your wrists ached and your eyes were killing you.

Karl felt that way now. He'd worn glasses ever since he was twelve, and his poor eyesight had been the one thing that might have disqualified him from the Mars program. He'd been fitted with extended wear contact lenses, but they made his eyes burn if he spent too much time reading.

Two things had been bothering Karl lately. One was trying to figure out what made Ian McShane tick. That was why Karl had been running microfiche, learning Irish history. He'd just gotten to the Easter Rebellion of 1916 when he realized he had ten minutes to report to the bridge. He'd been rushing through the commissary when he heard Ian mention his brother.

His brother who had died. It must have been something violent, Karl thought. Maybe something to do with the situation in Northern Ireland that was always on TV back home. That would explain about Ian and his attitude. Karl had felt the same way after his mother died. Maybe if Ian knew they had that much in common, he would get off his case.

He could ask Lanie, Karl thought. Lanie knew everything there was to know about Ian. But Lanie didn't like Karl any more now than she had when they first met in Houston.

Ian McShane was the first thing that was bothering Karl. The second was why Dr. Allen was so dissatisfied with him lately.

Everything he did seemed to be inadequate. His reflexes weren't fast enough. His systems checks weren't thorough enough. His instrument readings weren't accurate enough. Dr. Allen made him repeat some procedures over and over again, even though he'd been doing them on his own since they'd left Icarus, to improve his timing and accuracy.

"You run this kind of instrumentation long enough, you think you're good enough. Well, you aren't!" Dr. Allen would snap, not at all her usual cheerful self, handing Karl a clipboard with a list of errors he'd made on his last shift. "Maybe you never will be. Now run it again, and again, until you're perfect. Not almost perfect — perfect!"

"Sounds like a bloody drill sergeant!" Ian had whispered, sticking up for Karl for once. Dr. Allen heard him.

"And as for you, McShane — !"

She had chewed him out for a full ten minutes that time. But she was always chewing Ian out. He deserved it, Karl thought. He was late, he was arrogant, and he never did anything according to procedures. Whereas I, Karl thought, always do everything precisely according to procedures. Why is Dr. Allen picking on me?

He wouldn't ask her. It would sound like whining, and Karl was not a whiner. Instead, he worked twice as hard to be twice as good. But flying the ship wasn't fun anymore. Whenever he was on the bridge, his face wore the same grim expression, like a mask. He couldn't wait for this voyage to be over.

"We have two obstacles between us and the surface of Mars," Dr. Allen said at the next general briefing. "One is the actual soft landing itself. But before we can even think about that, there's the asteroid belt."

She waited for the murmurs to die down.

"I know what you're going to say. You're going to tell me that you studied all about the major belt between Mars and Jupiter, and how it isn't nearly as scary as we once thought it was, how there are sometimes thousands of miles between areas of debris, and you're right. You'll also tell me that if there is a smaller belt between us and Mars, it's probably no more than a stray fist-size rock and a handful of dust now and then. Nothing mountain-size, nothing scary.

"Well, I want to congratulate all of you for doing your astronomy homework, but I also want you to be aware that dust and debris can be lethal. No area of space is a complete vacuum, and no space vessel is ever completely safe. Our E.V.A. crews can tell you about the minor damage they've seen already. At the speed we're traveling, a micro-meteorite the size of a pebble can impact like a forty-five caliber slug. So while we're not all doomed to be eaten by the 'great galactic ghoul,' as it was once called, we're not entirely out of the woods yet either."

"How much danger is there?" someone shouted from the back of the rec room.

"If I told you the odds on your getting into an auto accident, you might never set foot in a car again,"

Dr. Allen said, and there was some nervous laughter. Only Karl didn't laugh; his grim face got even grimmer. "All right, you know what I mean. None of us will be riding in a conventional auto for a long time, though we will have Mars-rovers, and I expect some of you will be hot-rodding all over the area not too long from now. But we've ridden in cars on Earth, in spite of the danger, and we all survived. Considering the streamlined construction of these ships, the Blaster up front, and our constant checks of the exterior, we'll be in no more danger than passing through a hailstorm. To be on the safe side, we will maintain continuous radio contact with the *Nina* and *Pinta* until we are through the areas where the Mariner and Viking missions reported the heaviest concentrations of debris. And I expect our entertainment committee will have something planned once we make it through!"

There was a round of applause for Nathan, who really needed it. The cast had come off his ankle that morning; bones knit incredibly fast without the drag of gravity. For the first time since his stupid move with the skateboard, he felt like one of the crew again.

"We'll do our best!" he promised as Gen grinned at him, and Ian pounded him on the back, yelling "Right!"

"Battle stations, battle stations, all hands to battle stations . . ." Gen chanted as the briefing broke up and everyone floated back to work or sleep or recreation. "Shields up, go to yellow alert. This is not a

120

drill. Repeat: this is not a drill."

Alice looked at Noemi, who looked at Tara, who looked at Lanie, who looked at Lisette.

"Shut up, Gen!" the girls all shouted at once.

Chapter Nine

Most of the crew tried not to think about the asteroids. They went about their everyday routines and tried not to look at the vid screens, where the E.V.A. cameras showed a constant scan of the outer hull. Still, there was an odd kind of quiet over everything.

People talked in whispers, and didn't laugh as much or as loudly as usual. Music and video-game noises in the rec room were sometimes replaced by a nervous silence. Everyone knew that except for certain areas of engineering, you couldn't hear something hitting the outer hull, but everyone seemed to be listening anyway. Some of the pioneers reported trouble sleeping, or weird nightmares where they were suffocating or falling endlessly through space.

"I can't wait until this is over!" Sergei confided to Nathan as the entertainment committee planned the after-the-asteroid party. "Do you realize if any one of our three ships was damaged, it could endanger the entire expedition?"

"Hey, lighten up, Sergei," Nathan said distractedly, calculating the amount of refreshments they'd need.

Last time there hadn't been enough popcorn to go around.

Sergei was usually the life of every gathering. Always cheerful, always charming, he didn't seem to have any enemies, if you didn't count the broken-hearted girls. The boys trusted him and dug his sense of humor; the girls found him irresistible, or at least "cute." Even if his flirting sometimes made them furious, no one could stay mad at Sergei for long.

Lately, though, he had seemed moody and preoccupied. It wasn't only the stress everyone was feeling over the asteroids, Nathan decided. Sergei had even stopped playing chess, which had always been his second passion, after girls. He did his work, reported for exercise, then disappeared—either back in his quarters to sleep more than usual, or somewhere else where no one could find him. He'd even, Nathan realized with a jolt, stopped flirting. This could be serious.

"Hey, Sergei? Are you all right?"

Sergei's answer came a little too quickly. His grin was a little too forced.

"Of course, my friend. Why do you ask?"

"I'm not sure. You seem real quiet lately."

Sergei shrugged. "Concern about the asteroids? Or perhaps I am growing up at last? Maybe it's the Russian soul. We Russians frequently get melancholy for no reason. But I'm fine, Nathan, truly. And I thank you for your concern."

"It's not still about Ludmilla, is it?"

Sergei's grin faded. "You must be psychic. Yes, it's Ludmilla. She sends me messages almost daily. She talks as if we are engaged, Nathan. All because I flirted with her a long time ago in Leningrad. I don't want to be engaged, Nathan! I'm too young to die!"

"Why don't you tell her?" Nathan said. "It's crazy to plan that far ahead. None of us is going to have time for personal commitments for years yet. We've got a colony to set up. Explain that to her."

"It isn't just Ludmilla," Sergei admitted. "She's part of it, but I've been thinking about my life lately. Until now I have prided myself on being cool and in control where girls are concerned. Sometimes, like with Lisette, I forget that they have feelings too. Maybe I need to change my attitude."

Alice had arrived to see if the committee needed any new ideas for decorations.

"They say if you're about to die, your whole life flashes in front of you," she said without thinking. She saw the look on Sergei's face. "Sorry. I don't know where that came from. Seriously, Sergei, maybe you're just homesick or something."

"Maybe." Sergei shrugged again. "Listen, can you manage without me for a while? I have some thinking to do."

Alice and Nathan watched him go, concerned.

The bad news spread like wildfire.

"The *Nina*'s in trouble . . . we were on the radio and we lost contact . . . it may have lost the Canopus lock . . . we can't reestablish communications . . . the *Nina*'s in trouble . . ."

"Say again, *Nina*." Tara tried to speak calmly into

124

her headset. Her heart was pounding so hard she could barely hear, even if there was nothing to hear but static. "Repeat: we are no longer receiving you, *Nina*. Please come in. *Nina,* this is *Santa Maria.* We have lost contact. Please respond . . ."

She had been alone on capcom when the first call came in during their regular ship-to-ship check-in. It wasn't a distress call exactly, only Dr. Thompson's usual calm voice from the *Nina* saying that there might be a problem.

"Roger, *Santa Maria.* We think may have picked up some debris which is impacting on navcon. Running systems checks now to deter—"

Then the message had ended. Dr. Allen had been listening in from the flying bridge. Now she opened the shipwide intercom to let everyone know what was going on. She wanted those who could help to be on the alert, and she wanted to stop the rumors before they caused a panic.

Dr. Al-Wahab came immediately to the bridge after yanking Lanie off her break to meet him and several others from his crew there. Ian reached over and squeezed Lanie's hand from the copilot's seat.

"*Nina,* stay with us," Dr. Allen was saying over her headset. She sounded in control; only Karl, who had been offshift but came to the bridge to see what he could do, saw how white her knuckles were on the controls. "Repeat: *Nina,* we are no longer receiving you. Do not end transmission. Keep the frequency open, *Nina.* We will continue to broadcast. If you can still read us, signal on any frequency . . ."

There was still nothing but static.

"Damn!" Dr. Allen exclaimed. No one had ever heard her say anything that strong before. She unbuckled her restraint harness. Dr. Al-Wahab automatically took over for her. "Tara, is the *Pinta* still talking to the *Nina?* Lanie—get on the computer and see if we can pick them up on ship-to-ship interface."

Tara didn't speak for several minutes while she listened, first for the *Nina,* then for *Pinta,* her fingers playing over the comm board. Lanie's fingers were busy on the computer.

"Affirmative on computer interface, Dr. Allen." The words were out of her mouth before she realized how professional she sounded. No one on the bridge looked more surprised than Lanie. "We can still talk to the *Nina* on the computer."

"We've lost audio." Tara shook her head. "The *Pinta's* still broadcasting the same as we are, but the *Nina's* not answering. Or else it is answering, but neither we nor the *Pinta* can hear."

Karl looked at Ian, who looked back at Karl. Their usual differences were forgotten in an instant.

"The Canopus lock," they both said at once.

"How would that affect communications?" Tara frowned. She held her headset to one ear so she could hear what was going on around her as well.

"If your navigation's off, you can't aim your radio transmissions at the proper coordinates," Dr. Allen said. "The *Nina* may or may not be receiving us, but if its navcon's out, it can't answer back. Ali?"

Dr. Al-Wahab shook his head. "Possible, of course. But they should be able to correct it themselves within a few minutes. I suggest we don't panic."

"What if they can't fix it themselves?" Ian spoke out of turn. "You wouldn't mind if Karl and I ran some specs on the engineering computer to see what the problems could be?"

"I will tell you without looking at it that there's only one area of navcon that's exposed enough to be affected by debris. And the *Nina* can shake that out itself. We'll have it back on line within minutes, you'll see."

"Mind if we run specs on it anyway?" Ian snapped, adding at the last minute: "Sir?"

Dr. Al-Wahab shrugged. "If Dr. Allen can spare you . . ."

"Go!" she said immediately, if only to end a potential argument. She was leaning over Lanie's shoulder at the computer. "Break in on the *Nina*'s computer. Tell them to cut all unnecessary chatter and keep this channel open. Tell them to open another channel to the *Pinta*. Until they solve their comm problem, this is our only way to talk to them."

"Gotcha!" Lanie sounded more like her old self this time. She was already hacking in overrides to break into the *Nina*'s system.

For the next several hours, the *Santa Maria* was able to broadcast to the *Nina* through Tara on the radio, but the *Nina* could answer back only through Lanie on the computer. Sometimes the *Pinta* would break into communications as well, and Tara and her relief, a boy named Jonathan, were kept busy fielding calls from them without losing their cool. Dr. Allen worked as liaison between Lanie and Tara, reading Dr. Thompson's messages describing what was wrong with his ship from Lanie's computer monitor, calling down to Dr. Al-Wahab in engineering, who would instruct Tara what to radio back. This complicated form of communication was driving everyone nuts.

"And if they don't find out what's wrong with the *Nina* and fix it, we could all be in trouble," Lisette said solemnly, sipping hot chocolate with her crewmates in The Hub Café.

"How do you figure that?" Nathan asked.

Ever since the distress call from the *Nina,* no one aboard the *Santa Maria* seemed able to relax or even sleep; people got off their work shifts and simply hung around. There was a run on the hot chocolate dispenser and snack stations. They all spoke in whispers.

"Figure this," Lisette said, drawing little invisible designs on the countertop with her fingers. "If they can't fix what's wrong with the *Nina,* she'll have to be evacuated. We'd have to divide her crew between us and the *Pinta.*"

"They'll get her fixed," Nathan said confidently. "It's probably a minor problem. Some dust in a mechanism causing a glitch. As soon as they go E.V.A. and find it, they're back in business."

"Suppose they can't?" Noemi asked softly. "We've barely enough room for the crew we have. And we may be able to stretch the food and water rations, but you can't stretch oxygen. Besides—"

"—if we had to abandon the *Nina* and leave her adrift with all her own supplies on board—" Alice added.

"—not to mention the equipment and modular units for constructing the colony—" Sergei threw in.

"—we'd put a serious strain on our resources once we got to Mars," Noemi concluded. "Statistically, we'd have a 33.3 percent greater chance of failing as a colony."

They all lapsed into silence.

"You guys have it all figured out, don't you?" Nathan accused them. "You sit around inputting all this stuff on your PCs and creating your little theoretical models, while over on the *Nina* they're sweating the real stuff—"

"Cool down!" Alice warned him, punching him on the arm to get his attention. He'd been getting awfully loud. "We have to do something to keep ourselves from going nuts while we wait."

"This expedition was designed to consist of three interdependent ships," Noemi went on as if Nathan hadn't interrupted their train of thought. "If one ship doesn't make it, it puts the entire expedition in jeopardy. It's a stupid system, if you ask me—"

"No one asked you!" Nathan nearly shouted. He couldn't stand the negative vibes that were spreading everywhere. "I'm telling you, it's a minor problem. They'll fix it."

"And if they don't?" Lisette insisted.

"Well, figure this," Nathan said, throwing her own words back at her. "You want worst-case scenarios, I'll give you one. If the *Nina* can't readjust its attitude and regain the Canopus lock, it won't be able to steer. Even if everything else aboard the ship is functional, it can travel, but it won't know where it's going with any kind of accuracy. It could get too close to Mars's gravity well and get sucked down into the atmosphere like

129

a rock. Or it could miss Mars entirely and drift in space forever.

"Besides which," he added gloomily, "realistically, there's no way to evacuate the *Nina* anyway. Think about that."

No one had thought of that. In the movies and on TV these things were always possible.

"We'll use the workpods!" Sergei said brightly.

Each of the three ships carried two small workpods, E.V.A. shuttles designed for maintenance and repairs on an inflight vessel. They were never used in place of the pressure suits unless absolutely necessary, because they used too much fuel and oxygen.

"How big is a workpod, Sergei?" Nathan asked practically.

"Okay, it's designed to hold four persons maximum," the Russian boy admitted. "But if you pulled out the seats—"

Nathan shook his head. "You'd still be able to cram in only about eight, and you wouldn't have sufficient oxygen. And at the distance the *Nina* is from us and the *Pinta* right now, and continuing to drift—"

"Even with our pods and the *Pinta*'s working at maximum, the fuel would run out, or the *Nina* would drift out of range before we could evacuate more than a few people," Noemi finished for him. She had calculated it in her head while they were arguing.

The silence this time seemed to last forever.

"So either the *Nina* gets fixed, or we lose her," Lisette said, looking down at her hands. "With everyone aboard."

"It has to be a simple answer, it has to be!" Ian shouted in frustration, running his gloved hands through his spiky hair. "Look, Karl, run it again. It can't be anything but the 404A-sector housing. They've sucked up a little dust and it's screwed up their navcon. It's the only answer."

"That seems to be correct," Karl admitted. He was as stressed out as Ian, but he wouldn't let it show. Their two heads were so close together at the computer, they would have bumped if either moved too quickly. "But Dr. Al-Wahab says it's impossible."

"Dr. Al-Wahab could be wrong!" Ian protested. "I hate to break it to you, Sieg—Karl, but adults *can* be wrong."

Karl started to object, but then he smiled instead.

"You're right. Forgive me if I'm not as skeptical of authority as you are."

"We'll bring you around!" Ian elbowed him in the ribs, using the momentum to push off from the computer terminal. "I'm going to talk to Dr. Al-Wahab."

"No!" Karl pushed himself off too. Ian stopped and stared at him. "Let me. He expects trouble from you. He might be more willing to listen if it's me."

Ian laughed and motioned Karl to go up to the flying bridge ahead of him. "So now you're a diplomat too! Sister Mary Frances, Karl, I'm beginning to like you!"

Dr. Al-Wahab had troubles of his own.

"Now we've lost the computer interface as well," he

told both boys bleakly, turning away from the computer, where Lanie was desperately tapping in messages that weren't being answered. "Dr. Thompson's last message said they were beginning to spin. That means they can't go E.V.A. on their own vessel, either with the pressure suits or the workpods. Once there's a certain amount of instability, the computer automatically freezes the airlocks."

"So they can't get out and fix what's wrong even if they know what it is," Ian said glumly. "Karl, tell him what we've worked out."

Karl explained what the two of them had been thinking. Dr. Al-Wahab listened quietly, then shook his head.

"I am surprised at you, Karl. This does not indicate clear thinking. Look . . ." He unrolled an old-fashioned schematic of the three ships' basic design, kept in storage in case of massive computer failure. "The unit you're describing has triple redundancy backups, as does every critical mechanism aboard. In other words, if this fails here"—he poked the schematic with his finger—"this and this automatically take over to keep the mechanism functioning."

"What if this and this also fail?" Ian demanded, also poking the schematic with his finger.

"Impossible," Dr. Alwahab said. "The odds against it—"

"—are astronomical," Karl interrupted, surprising everyone. "I agree, sir. But what else could explain a combination of navcon failure, loss of communications, and now increased instability?"

"I don't know," Dr. Al-Wahab admitted. "But it can't

be anything as simple as you describe. We will have to run more tests."

Karl kept his voice level, though inside he was boiling. He must control his temper, must think clearly. Out of the corner of his eye he could see Dr. Allen watching him, though she didn't say a word. Suddenly he realized why she'd been down on him all these weeks. It was to prepare him to cope with just such an emergency as this.

Karl's mother had always taught him to control his temper.

Always count to ten before you speak. Take a deep breath, let it out, and you will find that the thing which made you angry is suddenly less important. Try it, Karlchen. You will see."

Mutti had hardly ever lost her temper, Karl remembered. At last he was mature enough to understand why. He counted to ten and studied Dr. Al-Wahab's schematic.

"Sir, I realize the odds are against it. But suppose what I'm suggesting has happened?"

"Then Dr. Thompson and his crew would have only so many options. From inside the ship they can manipulate these units here, and here, to try to get the navcon up and functional again. In fact, knowing Dr. Thompson. I'm certain he's already tried that."

"So that means he's run out of options." Ian butted in. "He's got to get help from outside."

Dr. Allen spoke for the first time.

"What are you suggesting?"

"That Karl and I climb into a workpod and go over and have a look-see," the Irish boy said, as if it weren't a trip of several hundred kilometers through space.

133

"Out of the question!" Dr. Al-Wahab exploded, losing his cool for the first time in anyone's memory. "Two trainees alone in a workpod over that distance? You'd have barely enough fuel to get there and back. An adult must go along. Assuming your theory is correct, we have an obligation to go over and try to help. The *Pinta*'s too far out of range. But you two, of all people, are not going together. I will choose one of you, and—"

"No, Ali," Dr. Allen said. Everyone stared at her. "Let them go alone. We need you here, and these two are the best pilots I've got. They're also crack engineers, even if their approaches are completely opposite. Maybe that's what's needed here, two sides of the coin. One can see what the other can't. Besides, we haven't brought them this far and trained them as adults in order to start treating them like children now."

Dr. Al-Wahab gestured at Karl and Ian. "But these two! They'll kill each other!"

Dr. Allen shrugged.

"Then that's two less we'll have to feed," she said, only half joking.

"What've we got to lose?" Ian demanded.

"Please, sir?" Karl asked reasonably.

"You will remain in constant contact with me," Dr. Al-Wahab instructed them as they hurried toward the E.V.A. airlock and the workpod. "You will provide me with a constant computer feed on your coordinates, and you will promise me not to do anything reckless

134

or stupid."

"Of course not, sir," Karl said.

"Trust us!" Ian grinned, and Karl suppressed a groan.

The after-the-asteroids party had been postponed indefinitely. No one had the heart to take the banner down. It flapped sadly against the bulkhead every time someone new drifted into the rec room.

"This place looks like a funeral parlor," Gen remarked, coming in for a break before he relieved Tara on comm. No one even bothered telling him to shut up.

"We shouldn't be hanging around here," Sergei said, though he didn't move. "We should be getting some sleep. Staying on the alert in case the *Nina*'s crew needs us."

"Needs us to do what?" Nathan asked. "Face it, Karl and Ian are the only ones who can do anything. All the rest of us can do is sit and wait."

"Hey, Nathan, look at it this way!" someone shouted from near the video games. "This way Suki Long won't get to Mars ahead of you. In fact, Suki may not get to Mars at all!"

Nathan propelled himself across the room toward his tormentor. He wanted to grab the wise-mouth by the throat. Was it his fault he'd been thinking exactly that, and feeling guilty at the same time? Could anyone blame him for wondering what it would be like if the *Nina* drifted off into space, and he never had to deal with Suki again? But no one had the right to say it out loud.

Nathan hated to fight. But he was ready to beat the other boy's face in, and it must have shown on his own face. The wise-mouth's friends gathered around him, and halfway across the rec room Nathan realized he was hopelessly outnumbered. Still, he had to defend his honor.

"That's none of your business!" he shouted, too late to stop his momentum anyway.

But someone suddenly moved between him and the wise-mouth.

"Cool down," Dr. Allen said sharply. "And settle down, all of you. There's something I have to say."

Chapter Ten

"We never tried to kid you about the potential danger," Dr. Allen began. She had opened the intercom to address not only those gathered in the rec room but those who couldn't leave their posts. "Each of you knew there were risks. That's why you and your parents had to sign so many forms before you left Earth. We hoped we would never run into anything like what's happened to the *Nina,* but we have, and there it is.

"There's nothing most of us can do but wait out this crisis. But that doesn't mean we have to do nothing. It will take Karl and Ian approximately three hours in the workpod to reach the *Nina.* Until then, maintain your normal routines. Thank you." Dr. Allen signed off and faced Nathan and the others. "And we can help each other by discussing things calmly."

"Oh, no!" Sergei groaned. "Is this going to be one of those get-in-touch-with-your-feeling sessions?"

"Do you have a problem with that?" Dr. Allen wanted to know.

Sergei looked embarrassed. "Well, yes. I mean, it's pointless. Talking about our feelings won't help the people on the *Nina*."

"That's true," Dr. Allen admitted. "But this is what we've done. We've notified Mission Control of what's happened. There's nothing they can do directly, because the *Nina*'s drifted too far off course for them to manipulate the navcon unit by remote from Earth. But they have run systems checks and confirmed that it is the 404A unit which has malfunctioned, just as Ian guessed."

"So once the two of them get there, they can fix it!" Alice said hopefully.

"Maybe," Dr. Allen said. "Maybe not. We're hoping against hope that nothing happens, but if it does—"

"Talking about the possibilities could help us to deal with them before they happen," Noemi interrupted. "After all, statistically, some of us are supposed to die before this colony is fully established anyway."

Her words cast a chill over the entire room.

" 'Supposed to' die?" Dr. Allen repeated.

"Statistical probability isn't really my field," Noemi said, absently tossing her long hair. Knowing she had everyone's attention helped her focus her thoughts. "But it is a fact that out of any given population, a certain percentage will die of disease, accidents, and so forth. Our group is unique in that we're all young and in exceptional physical conditions. So normal stats don't apply. But the danger of our being killed in an accident are proportionately greater . . ."

"I'm relieving you," Gen said, prying the headset out of Tara's hands. "Beat it. Get some sleep."

"I'm not tired!" Tara yawned.

"No, of course not," Gen said. "You've been on comm, trying to raise the *Nina* for three hours straight, and you were onshift for two hours before that. You haven't eaten, slept, or even gone to the bathroom. And I didn't see you yawn just now. You must be Superwoman."

"I can hang in for a while longer."

"If you were your supervisor, how would you rate your efficiency right now?" Gen reasoned.

Tara surrendered. "The pits. Less than zero. You're right. I'm outta here. But you don't mind if I hang around and listen in, just in case?"

"Be my guest," Gen said, settling the headset over his ears. He could hear Karl reading off coordinates to Dr. Al-Wahab in his calm voice. The next time he looked over at Tara, she was attached to a wall panel, sound asleep.

"I'm asking you to do one thing when we get there," Ian said, sliding the bottom of his pressure suit over his long, skinny legs.

"What's that?" Karl asked from the workpod's controls.

"Be flexible. Don't always go by the book. We've already shown Dr. Al-Wahab this isn't a by-the-book situation. We're going to have to be creative."

"Like hot-wiring a car?" Karl asked.

"You got it!" Ian said.

"There it is!" Karl said suddenly, unable to keep the excitement out of his voice. "It hasn't drifted that far off course after all!"

He'd been flying the workpod on instruments, aim-

139

ing for where the *Nina* should have been if it had stayed on course. Now one small white dot began to separate itself from the star field, becoming the familiar cigar-shaped ship. Karl realized he and Ian would *have* to save the *Nina*. There was no room for failure.

"Pod One to *Santa Maria,*" Karl said into his headset. "Pod One to *Santa Maria*. We have a visual on *Nina*. Anticipate rendezvous in ten minutes — mark."

"Roger, Pod One," came Gen's voice after a several-second lag. "You guys haven't killed each other yet! Amazing!"

Ian laughed. Karl gave him a long-suffering look.

"*Santa Maria,* this is Pod One," he said tightly. "Suggest we keep this conversation to the basics, over."

"Sorry about that, Pod One." The two boys in the workpod could hear the laugh in Gen's voice. Then Dr. Al-Wahab was speaking to them.

"Pod One, can you give us a visual on *Nina?* How badly is it yawing, over?"

Their biggest worry had been whether or not the *Nina,* unable to control its navcon, would be spinning so fast on its vertical axis that they wouldn't be able to grapple the workpod onto it. Karl was busy with the thrusters, slowing the pod down. He nodded to Ian to do the talking.

"It seems to be moving rather leisurely. There's a definite yaw, but it must take it a full five minutes to do 360 degrees. We shouldn't have too much trouble getting alongside of her — over."

"Understood, Pod One. Do what you have to do, gentlemen. *Santa Maria* standing by."

" 'Standing by,' " Karl repeated. "I guess you and I have quite a reputation. This job will have to show

140

them we can work together."

"That and maybe an attitude change," Ian suggested.

"I'm not the one with the attitude—" Karl began, then mentally counted to ten. "Look, I know about you. About how the priests saved you from a life of crime. About your brother in prison, and the one who died. Do you know anything about me but what you see? If I told you my mother also died senselessly, in an auto accident, would you care?"

Karl was breathing hard, but he kept his eyes on the *Nina* ahead of them.

"I didn't know, sport. I'm sorry," Ian said after a long moment. "Can I tell you something else?"

"What's that?" Karl checked his instrument readings against the ship before them, trusting nothing until he'd double-checked it.

"I noticed Dr. Allen's been on your case a lot lately. Hold on, don't bite my head off! D'you ever stop to think why?"

Karl fired the portside thruster to heel the workpod over parallel to the slowly rotating *Nina*.

"Obviously I am not doing my job well enough to please her," he said tightly.

"Not a bit of it," Ian said, reaching for the top half of his pressure suit.

Karl risked a brief glance in his direction.

"What do you mean?"

"You're the best pilot she's got." Ian gripped Karl's arm for emphasis. "Better'n me. Maybe better'n any of the trainees on any of the ships. That's why she's down on you, to make your best better. The way Father Stephen used to ride me all the time back home. 'Get your math scores up, you lazy scut! Get your eyes off

141

the girls and your mind off the football and practice those equations until they're engraved on your soul!' I wanted to kill him. We actually came to blows once, only it was him that knocked me down. Knocked some sense into me, too, because that's when I figured out what he was trying to do."

"And you think that's what Dr. Allen's doing to me," Karl said thoughtfully. His practiced touch on the controls caused the workpod to move in close enough to the *Nina*, even with the yaw, to extend a grapple.

"She doesn't have to knock you down, mate, for it to be the same thing," Ian said knowingly.

Everyone seemed to have forgotten about Lanie. She sat stubbornly hunched over her keyboard, staring at the blank computer monitor, hoping that the *Nina* would reestablish the computer interface. She looked up to find Lisette watching her.

"You scared me! How long have you been here?"

"A couple of minutes. What're you doing?"

"Wondering if I dare get off the screen long enough to try running some test schematics to see if I can figure out from here what the *Nina*'s problem is," she explained. "The 404A has something like twenty subunits, and it would save time for Karl and Ian if I could figure out which one is the glitch."

"Someone else could mind the screen while you did that," Lisette suggested. She began getting into one of the engineering PCs. "I'm not as good as you, but I could do that."

Lanie thought it over, then nodded. "That way I can run the schematics. Thanks. I appreciate it."

Both girls got to work. It was better than doing nothing.

Dr. Allen was in the rec room doing her bit for ship's morale. Dr. Al-Wahab was standing by on the radio with Karl and Ian in the workpod. That meant Dr. Berger was piloting the *Santa Maria,* and Alice was in charge of the hydroponics lab. She was grateful to keep busy, but she couldn't keep her mind from working overtime.

The *Santa Maria* was clear of the so-called asteroid belt now. The *Pinta* had reported in that it, too, was clear. If they could only get the *Nina* fixed, Alice thought, absently feeding nutrients to a row of young broccoli, everything would be fine! A tear slid down Alice's cheek. In the lab's artificial gravity, it didn't float off in midair, but stayed.

There were tears in the rec room, too, even from some of the boys. Sergei was right. Dr. Allen had led them into a get-in-touch-with-your-feelings session. But Dr. Allen was right too. Instead of hurting, it helped. Even Sergei was sniffling a little.

"The worst thing we can do," Dr. Allen was saying, "is pretend nothing's wrong with the *Nina,* and it's all going to go away by some kind of magic; then we won't be prepared for any other contingency. That's not saying we have to fall into a lot of gloom and doom, but I'd like each of you to think of what you might do if you were the expedition's leader, or if you were aboard the *Nina.* What decisions would you make, and how do you think

143

they would affect others? Volunteers?"

Does that mean *she* isn't sure? Nathan wondered. Dr. Allen's an adult; she's been put in charge because of her ability to make life or death decisions. If she has doubts, where does that put the rest of us? His hand went up before he could stop himself.

"Nathan?"

"We've discussed this already, but the most serious thing that can happen is that we can't get the *Nina* fixed and we have to let it drift. Suppose we could evacuate it? We could work out an exchange, with some of us from the *Santa Maria* and the *Pinta* swapping over, since we couldn't double up and still have enough oxygen. Maybe we could even rig a kind of piggyback, take it in tow. But how do we decide whom to leave behind."

"If you were the expedition's leader, Nathan, what do you think you would do?" Dr. Allen asked.

"I think the best thing to do would be to draw lots. A completely random drawing that everybody would have to agree on beforehand. Let the computer do it, say, or—"

"That's dumb!" the wise-mouth who had been taunting Nathan about Suki shouted. "That's so totally stupid! What if all your pilots ended up in the group that had to stay behind? Or all your hydroponics experts?"

"The odds against that—" Noemi started to say.

"The only fair way is to get rid of the people who are least essential to the success of the expedition and the colony," the same boy said. "We don't really need theoretical mathematicians. Or rock collectors," he said, pointing at Sergei. "Or all-around skateboard nerds who aren't that good at anything!"

This went back to the incident with the hydroponics

144

lab, reminding Nathan once again that he might never live it down. He suddenly remembered that this boy had been very friendly with Suki before they left Icarus, and had been really bummed out when they were assigned separate ships. Nathan touched Sergei and Noemi on the shoulder to keep them from shouting back at the troublemaker.

"A lot of us have friends aboard the *Nina*," Nathan said, refusing to get angry. "Maybe we're wondering why they should be in danger while we're safe. Nobody's saying it's fair. But how do you put a value on a human life? What are you, some kind of Nazi or something? What gives you the right to play God?"

Ian crawled out from under the workpod's communications console, a ratchet screwdriver in one hand.

"Try it now." He nodded at Karl.

"*Nina*, this is Workpod One," Karl said. "We have patched our comm system onto yours and compensated for the yaw. You should be able to get through to the *Santa Maria* via us—over. Dr. Thompson, can you read us?"

There was a great deal of static, then a voice.

"Workpod One, Suki Long here. To whom am I speaking?"

"Sister Mary Frances!" Ian said. "Isn't that perfect?"

"Karl Muller here, Suki."

"And Ian McShane, Suk. How's tricks?"

Both boys could hear Suki gasp. Whether she was overjoyed because they had comm again, or horrified to learn who her rescuers were, neither could tell.

"McShane, I wish I could say I was glad to hear from

you . . ." she began, but Dr. Thompson interrupted her.

"Glad to hear from you, guys. Can you confirm whether we have comm with the *Santa Maria?*"

As if on cue, Genshiro's voice came through loud and clear.

"Roger, *Nina*, we have a fix and an open channel. Will try to compensate as you yaw. *Santa Maria* standing by."

"I don't mean to be a damp blanket—" Karl began.

"That's 'wet blanket,' sport," Ian corrected him.

"Whatever. But we have work to do."

He had brought the workpod as close as he could alongside the navcon housing. Now he and Ian would have to go E.V.A. and work on the problem hands-on.

"Understood, Workpod One," Dr. Thompson said. "Is there anything we can do by remote from in here?"

"Sure," Ian answered. "Scare us up a wire coat hanger, and ask Suki if she's still got any chewing gum. We'll have your navcon up in no time!"

"It's working, Dr. Allen!" Gen shouted gleefully over the intercom so the whole ship could hear. "The *Nina*'s tied in with our com again!"

A cheer went up from the rec room. When Dr. Allen could hear again, she spoke to Gen.

"Great! Keep the intercom open, and relay the news to the *Pinta*. Stay on that frequency, Genshiro. Don't go to sleep on me!

"It's not over yet, people," she told the crowd in the rec room, who had started to settle down "All this means is that we can talk to the *Nina* again. The serious problem remains to be solved."

"And if it isn't solved within the next two hours," Noemi reported, having consulted with some of the other mathematicians over a keyboard, "it'll be too late anyway. The *Nina* will have drifted too far off its trajectory to get back on again. And our workpod will have to let go or it won't have enough fuel to return."

The room settled into an uneasy silence.

"You didn't have to tell them that!" Nathan whispered furiously.

"They deserve to know!" Noemi shot back. "We're supposed to be facing reality, right?"

"Let's get back to our discussion," Dr. Allen suggested. "Sergei? You were going to say something when we were interrupted."

The Russian boy shook his head.

"It's not important. I was only going to say that a leader should never ask his crew to do something he wouldn't do." His voice cracked with emotion. "If we could somehow evacuate the *Nina* and had to leave some people behind, I would volunteer to stay so that others might live!"

No one expected the usually easygoing Sergei to say anything so serious. Nathan suddenly saw his friend in a whole new light. There was more discussion of what Sergei had said, until a burst of static from the intercom silenced everyone. The voice that came through was not from the *Nina*. It was Karl.

"The mechanism's been damaged beyond repair. The *Nina* can't get her airlocks open to send us a replacement, and we haven't enough fuel or oxygen to get to the *Santa Maria* and back before it drifts farther. There's nothing we can do!"

Chapter Eleven

"There's a pebble the size of my thumbnail," Karl reported on the open frequency so all three ships could pick it up. "It's somehow gotten past the navcon housing and rattled around inside the mechanism, cutting through one of the O rings. Without the O ring, the binary between the navcon computer and the aft portside thruster shuts down automatically. In other words—"

"In other words, without a replacement O ring we can't tell the thruster when to fire," Dr. Thompson finished Karl's thought for him. "Even if we could override the navcon from here, we wouldn't get a trajectory reading. And a yaw of a few degrees at this distance could put us a thousand kilometers off course."

"I'm afraid so, sir," Karl said.

"A forty-five-caliber bullet," Ian was saying, his hands on either side of the striation the tiny rock had made along the heat-resistant tiles before ricocheting around inside the navcon unit.

"What?" Karl wasn't sure he'd heard correctly over his headset. He couldn't see Ian's face through the helmet visor, and his mind was racing with possible ways to fix the navcon. He remembered that it was something as simple as a malfunction of the O rings that had caused the *Challenger* shuttle to explode in 1986. The little things were important.

"A forty-five-caliber bullet," Ian repeated. "Dr. Allen said a pebble that size would have the impact of a bullet. A bullet like the one that killed my brother!"

Karl floated over to him on his restraint tether, gripping his spacesuited arm with his gloved hand.

"Don't think about that now! Remember what you told me: be flexible. There's got to be something inside the workpod that uses the same size O rings."

Ian shook his head. It made his helmet move only slightly.

"Afraid not, boyo. Like you said, there's nothing we can do."

Karl gripped his arm tighter. " 'If it's broke, Ian Mc-Shane can fix it,' " he reminded his companion.

Ian's face went blank for a moment behind his polarized visor. Suddenly he gripped Karl's shoulders and both boys shouted at once: "The atmospheric control unit!"

Together they used the handholds along the *Nina*'s hull to push themselves back toward the waiting workpod. Dr. Thompson's voice interrupted them while they were opening the hatch:

"I don't know, boys. That might not be a good idea—"

"The specs are the same, guys," a new voice cut in, interrupting Dr. Thompson as if he hadn't spoken. It was Lanie, transmitting from the *Santa Maria;* with the time lag she wouldn't hear Dr. Thompson for a few seconds more. "I've run 'em through the computer, and Dr. Al-Wahab confirms. The O rings on a workpod ACU and those on the main navcon-to-thruster binary are both four point five centimeters in diameter."

"Roger, Lanie. We can't talk now!" Ian radioed her, diving into the workpod and pulling off his helmet just as Karl had the hatch closed.

"Workpod crew, if you scavenge your own space O rings, you have no backup for possible malfunction of your own vessel," Dr. Thompson said, even as Karl and Ian dove under the control panel to free up the unit, study the O rings, and find the correct size spare in the repair locker. "We won't let you risk that. Repeat—"

"We copy, *Nina*," Karl said crisply, as he and Ian rummaged through the locker. "But our risk is minimal. If our ACU goes, we have the pressure suits for backup. And there are only two of us, compared to one hundred thirty-five of you. We'll take the chance."

"Besides, Dr. Thompson," Ian cut in, one of the correct O rings already in his hand, "you know what Dr. Al-Wahab alway says—"

" 'Every unit has triple redundancy fail-safes!' " both boys said at once, trading high-fives before they slipped the O rings into their Velcro belt packs and opened the workpod's hatch.

The shouting and cheering as Karl and Ian returned safely through the *Santa Maria*'s airlock over four hours later was nearly deafening. Everyone on the ship wanted to touch them, clap them on the back, congratulate them in person. The party was back online, but the two heroes of the hour begged off. All they wanted, after seven grueling hours in a workpod and outside the *Nina*'s hull, was a shower and some sleep.

Everyone else who was not on duty ended up at the party, but it didn't turn out the way Nathan and his committee had planned it.

All three ships were now on course and through the last of the dust and debris. Within thirty days they would be in orbit around Mars. They were almost home free. But the after-the-asteroids party, which was supposed to be their last big celebration before the landing, somehow wasn't the raucous boogie the mid-point party had been.

The video games were silent. No one put on any tapes, and no one wanted to play. There was no dancing. Most people sat around talking quietly, too tired or too wired to sleep. No one wanted to leave, but no one wanted to make too much noise either.

"I'm exhausted!" Alice yawned. Her yawn became contagious, and soon everyone around her was yawning. Gen looked as if he were asleep sitting up. "Why should I be exhausted when I didn't do anything? Karl and Ian, Lanie and Gen and Tara did all the work. All I did was wait."

"Sometime's waiting's harder," Nathan said quietly.

"We're only now realizing how incredibly lucky we've been," was how Tara explained it. "We came very close to losing a lot of valuable people. It's made us think. Maybe that's why we don't want to rock the boat by making a lot of noise right now."

"We've also learned some things about ourselves, and about one another," Nathan said, thinking of Sergei, who was still awfully quiet.

"It's true," the Russian boy said. "I remember literature classes, and how the teacher was always babbling on about what makes heroes. And all those books we had to read. I used to think it was so much garbage, but now I realize people show their true colors in a crisis. We're all a little bit coward and a little bit hero. Only in a life-or-death situation do we find out who we really are."

"You're still my hero, Sergei!" Noemi teased, giggling.

"And you're my movie star!" Sergei said gallantly, tugging the single curl over her ear and giving her shoulder a squeeze. "When they remake *Doctor Zhivago*, I will play Yuri, and you can be my Lara."

"Get real!" Lanie said, making a disgusted face.

The laughter and joking went on until everyone was too tired to move. Dr. Allen ordered anyone who wasn't absolutely essential to go back to quarters and catch some Zs. Nobody argued.

"Good morning, *Santa Maria!*" Gen's SNAP *Morning Show* radio voice filtered throughout the entire ship. "We have this just in from Dr. Lawrence Thompson, our main man in navigational astrophysics straight from the *Nina's* flying bridge, who confirms that, yes, we will achieve Mars orbit at approximately 1330 hours—give or take an hour on two—seventeen days from now. To celebrate, Radio SNAP brings you this golden oldie from Deep Purple: 'Space Truckin'. . .'"

Alice passed by engineering to wave at Gen, who sat with his headset draped around his neck while the tape played. Nathan called her from the flying bridge.

"Want to see something?"

"What?" Alice asked, following him up.

She hardly ever came this far forward in the ship. She was almost always in the hydroponics lab, or inspecting the plants people still had growing in their quarters, which were taking on the most fantastic shapes in zero G. Seeing the stars through the bridge windshield instead of on a vid-screen, she gasped. Nathan wanted to show her something specific.

"Tell me what you see at approximately ten o'clock?"

Alice had to close her eyes and picture a clock face in her mind before she looked. Dr. Al-Wahab smiled at her from the pilot's seat as she leaned between him and Ian, her hand on Ian's shoulder.

"Something reddish. It's not a star. It's not twinkling."

"Mars," Nathan said. It gave Alice goose bumps.

"We're that close!" she found herself whispering. "It's real, isn't it? We're almost there!"

Tara handed Karl his beef Stroganoff, and some of Dr. Berger's fresh-picked broccoli hot from the microwave, and got herself a serving of granola with raisins. They were on opposite shifts, so her breakfast was Karl's dinner break.

"Lisette," she called. "Do you want something while I'm here?"

"Just tea, thanks. I've got to put in at least an hour on the bike. Don't want to do that on a full stomach."

"Lemon and sugar," Tara announced, handing the container to Lisette, who pulled up the straw and started to sip. "So, Karl. How does it feel to be a hero?"

The German boy looked grimmer than usual.

"I wish everyone would stop calling me that! What

153

Ian and I did was not heroic at all."

"Saving an entire ship full of people?" Tara asked, picking the raisins out of her granola and eating them first. "That sounds pretty heroic to me."

"We did only what we had to do," Karl insisted. "That's not heroism. Look, if you'd been out there with us, and you realized the whole problem could be fixed by replacing a couple of O rings, what would you do?"

"Replace the O-rings, of course," Tara said. "But that's not the point."

"I don't understand, then," Karl said. "What is the point?"

"The point is—oh, I don't know—it's not just a question of doing what needs to be done. It's being the person who needs to be there. Like Noemi figuring out how to upgrade the water recovery system—"

"Exactly!" Karl nodded. "Because she has the expertise in mathematics, she was the right person for the job. Because Ian and I are trained in engineering, we were the right people for the O-ring job."

"Also because you're a great team. Rule-Book Man and the Boy Rebel," Lisette stuck in. Everybody laughed.

Karl stopped spooning up his Stroganoff and smiled a little. He really has a great smile, Tara thought. Too bad he hardly ever uses it!

"You're right, of course. I'm sorry! But this idea of being a 'hero' . . ." Karl shook his head, picked up a stalk of broccoli, and began chewing. "It's hard. People expect you to be Superman all the time. Then if you make one little mistake, everyone gets down on you. I'd rather not have all that attention."

"Weird!" Lisette remarked, pushing off for her ergobike session.

"You are, you know," Tara said when she and Karl were alone.

Karl hunched his shoulders, embarrassed.

"Maybe. If it's strange to get satisfaction out of a job well done without needing to be praised for it as well, I guess I am weird."

"But nice" Tara added.

"It's worse than waiting for Christmas!" Noemi squealed, clapping her hands excitedly. "I can't wait, I really can't!"

"You could go E.V.A. and push," Gen suggested. Noemi made a "shut-up-Gen" face at him.

With so few days left, the waiting was killing them. It was harder than ever to stick to the routines, to get the work done, when everyone wanted to crowd up to the flying bridge and sneak a peek at the growing reddish blob that still seemed so unreal through the forward screen. Dr. Allen, always the good psychologist, solved the problem by assigning extra drills and departmental meetings.

At least once every shift there was an emergency suit-up drill to see how fast everyone could climb into their flight suits and hook up to the restraint harnesses after more than seven months in space. There were extra gym workouts too.

"Except for whatever time you've spent in the hydroponics lab, you've all been half a year in weightlessness," Dr Allen explained. "At one to two percent muscle loss per month, that means you're an average of six to twelve percent weaker than when you left Earth. It's normal, and we expected it. It means that even Mars, with its gravity at only thirty-eight percent of Earth's, is going to wear us out for a while until we adjust.

"More immediately, you'll start to feel the tug as soon as we enter Mars orbit, and we'll be decelerating into the atmosphere at anywhere from 11,000 to 17,500 miles per hour. That's going to put a lot of stress on arteries, bones, and muscles that have been spoiled by zero G. That's also why we're emphasizing suit-up drills, because if you're out of harness and you fall or bump into anything during entry . . ."

Dr. Allen let her voice trail off so everybody could figure out the consequences for themselves. When she saw everyone was paying attention, she went on.

"Bottom line: extra gym time. The stronger you are now, the better for you later."

Dr. Berger and the hydroponics trainees had been holding departmental meetings throughout the voyage. Now engineering and geology teams joined them for interdepartmental meetings. Today it was Sergei's turn to lead the discussion.

"The Mangala Vallis region—that's Latin for 'valley'—was targeted beforehand as the best location for a permanent colony," he began, pointing it out on a detailed wall map, sounding very professional. "It's got some of the most interesting topography on the planet. There's Olympus Mons, the largest known volcano in the solar system. There's the Valles Marineris region, which is a canyon over 2,400 miles long—"

"So the scenery's nice," Alice interrupted. "But what are the advantages in terms of survival?"

"It's close to the equator," Sergei pointed out, "which means daytime temperatures of as much as sixty degrees Fahrenheit or higher."

"Sounds positively tropical!" Tara remarked, pretending to shiver.

"Hey, in Leningrad that would be a heat wave !" Sergei said, breaking everyone up. "Okay, further reasons for choosing this area: if you look at the soil patterns, it's clear that there was once surface water, and the Viking soil samplers proved there is water in the rocks. And water is going to be our most important concern, after oxygen. Also, since this is a valley, with not only Olympus Mons but the rest of the Tharsis Ridge protecting it, there should be less hazard from dust storms. Martian dust storms can last for weeks. It would be nice to avoid them."

"Volcanos!" Lanie said. "Is it smart to start a colony near a volcano? What about boiling lava, earthquake faults, stuff like that?"

"Not from these babies," Sergei explained. "The volcanos have been studied, and they're all inactive. As for earthquakes, there has been no tectonic activity recorded on Mars since we began taking readings years ago. When it comes to seismic activity, Mars is safer than Earth."

"What about the soil?" Alice asked.

"From what the Viking scoops tell us, it seems to be of two major types," Sergei said. "The light yellowish stuff is ordinary sand, like what you'd find on a beach on Earth. The darker stuff is composed of limonite, similar to what we found on the moon, and hydrated ferrous oxide. What gives it the characteristic reddish color is actually a form of rust."

157

"And rust means oxygenation, which means an atmosphere," Lanie said. Gen and some of the others applauded her. She'd been doing her homework.

"Yes, but unfortunately, not a breathable atmosphere," Sergei apologized. "It's still mostly carbon dioxide."

"At least the plants will love it," Alice said. "And limonite is volcanic. Volcanic soil's the best for growing things."

"Okay, that's it for me," Sergei said, taking down his wall map and rolling it up.

"I just want to add one thing," Nathan said. "You forgot to mention the robot ships we sent ahead. They're in synchronous orbit above the Mangalla Vallis region, waiting for us. Once we've landed, we'll have to start ferrying down equipment and supplies from them."

It was becoming more real all the time. People were making plans, talking excitedly.

"It sounds as if you all know what to do," Dr. Al-Wahab said quietly.

"Now all we have to do," Lanie added, "is get there and do it!"

First the little reddish blob began to take on a definite shape. Its color deepened from a rusty pink to a deep red-orange with distinct darker and lighter patches. It continued to grow.

It grew to the size of a penny, then to the size of a compact disc, then to the size of a dinner plate, then to the size of a beach ball. It became a three-dimensional sphere, fat and inviting. The white polar caps became distinct. The dark patches transformed themselves into valleys and canyons and what looked like dry river beds. And Mars kept growing.

Soon it filled the E.V.A. screens. Then it filled the forward windshield, blocking out the stars.

Every few hours the tiny moon Phobos would fly by on its under-three-hour orbit. Less frequently, more slowly, and at a higher perigee, the second moon, Deimos, made its appearance. The young astronauts noticed them only in passing. Their eyes, their hearts, were full of Mars.

The E.V.A. cameras were rotated aft, and two more shapes became visible. Small, cigar-shaped, blindingly white on their sunward flanks, totally black in shadow, the *Nina* and *Pinta* were within visual range for the first time since all three had left the orbital space platform Icarus. They entered orbit one behind the other, so close they could read the lettering on each other's sides, so close that communication between ships was now instantaneous.

"Welcome to Mars, people!" Dr. Allen announced to all three ships.

"Roger, and thanks!" radioed the *Pinta*'s pilot, and Dr. Thompson answered from the *Nina:* "We have you in sight, *Santa Maria*. Preparing for first of multiple orbits. Firing thrusters in four minutes — Mark."

"Dr. Thompson will be 'talking us down' at about this time tomorrow," Dr. Allen explained to her crew. "Meanwhile, we'll be completing a series of planetary orbits, taking pictures and spectography readings, and running as many tests as we can in the time allotted to us."

"Why can't we soft-land now?" Noemi wanted to know.

"Because this is the only chance we'll have to do this," Nathan explained. "Once we land, most of us will be too busy to take the time to get this information."

"The First and Final Mars World Tour!" Gen announced happily, playing his air guitar. "We should have had T-shirts printed! Why didn't we think of it?"

"Shut up and enjoy the scenery!" Alice said, watching her new world go by.

"Awesome!" Sergei said.

"Totally!" Nathan agreed.

Chapter Twelve

"They don't look real!" was how Lanie described the robot ships with their multiple cargo pods, hanging like Christmas ornaments in geosynchronous orbit above the Mangala Valley.

"None of this looks real," Nathan agreed. "The first time we came around to nightside, I kept looking for city lights. It still hasn't gotten through to me that we'll be the first humans — the first anything — to set foot on this planet."

"Why are we whispering?" Lanie wondered.

"I don't know," Nathan said, and they both cracked up.

"Olympus Mons," Sergei said, pointing out the huge flattened cone as it passed beneath them. He'd been pointing out each topographical feature as it went by: "Chryse Planitia, the Plain of Chryse. Margaritifer Sinus, the Sea of Pearls. Xanthe. Lunae Planum, Plain of the Moon. Ceraunius Tholus — 'tholus' means 'hill.' And the Tharsis Ridge: Ascraeus Mons, Pavonis Mons, and Arsia Mons. And, last but not least: Mount Olympus, Martian-style. On Earth, Mount Olympus was the home of the Greek gods. On Mars, Olympus Mons is a volcanic crater seventeen miles high and 370 miles across. That's more than three times the height of Everest, and as wide as the state of Missouri."

"Incredible!" Noemi said.

"And if you look real close, you can see the 'canals,' " Nathan joked.

" 'Canals'?" Ian repeated. "Not real, man-made canals?"

Sergei was laughing. "That old myth! Come on, Nathan, explain it to our favorite pilot."

"In 1877 Schiaparelli first described a network of lines crisscrossing all the 'continents' of Mars, but it was Percival Lowell, an American, who decided they were too regular to be natural phenomenon and had to be man-made. Now we think it may have been an error in the refraction of the telescopes the men were using, or poor eyesight, or maybe just wishful thinking. But even as late as the 1950s science fiction writers were describing little green men, or monsters, who invaded San Francisco until they died of cold germs."

"But we're *so* much smarter these days," Sergei said a little smugly. "We now know that Mars has almost no atmospheric pressure. The atmosphere is so thin it's practically a vacuum, therefore liquid water cannot exist on the surface. Much less little green men."

"Except for Dr. Berger's," Alice chimed in. "We'll have to build pressure domes to grow our crops."

"And a soft landing on Mars will be different from one on Earth or even on the moon," Dr. Allen said, joining them. "Is anyone in the mood for one more practice drill?"

Everyone groaned. But they all trooped off to get their flight suits anyway.

Instant replay, Nathan thought as he hooked his flight-suit to the safety harness for the last time. This wasn't a drill; this was the real thing. Nathan turned from side to side to see the dozens of similar figures lining the corridors, in exactly the assigned positions they'd had when the *Santa Maria* left the Icarus space-dock. Except for the fact that this time they had atmosphere and wouldn't need their helmets until they began to power-down for the landing, everything looked exactly the same.

It's as if you rewound the video back to the beginning, Nathan thought. We're exactly where we started out. Noemi and Alice are across from me, Lanie's a little farther down next to Tara, Sergei's on my right, and Gen's way down there by the E.V.A. screen, with Lisette diagonally across from him. And Karl's in the copilot's seat again, with Dr. Allen piloting. *Déjà vu.*

We're right back where we started, only we're thirty-five million miles away. Not only in the actual distance we've traveled, but in how we've changed.

Look at Lanie and Tara, yakking and giggling as if they'd been friends for life, when a few months ago they hated each other. Noemi's upgraded design for the water recycler is going to be used on all future interplanetary vessels, Dr. Thompson says. He just got the approval from Geneva. There'll even be a patent in Noemi's name.

Not that we'll need money on Mars. Not that Noemi

163

would need money anyway, with her rich family. But it's a prestige thing. It says we're not kids anymore. We're doing things that make a difference.

Some people haven't changed much, Nathan thought. Alice is about the same, but then, Alice was together from the beginning. The same with Lisette. She and I are still tight, and she doesn't need to change a bit.

Then there's Gen, who's managed to loosen up and relate to people in his own crazy way, without ever losing an ounce of cool. If I didn't like him so much, Nathan thought, I'd probably envy him.

Then there's Karl and Ian. Talk about the Odd Couple. Who'd have thought a tough Irish street punk and stiff old Karl would become friends, but there it is. Dr. Allen said something about surviving a crisis together. Like being in a war or something. Or saving the *Nina* practically single-handed. It changes people. Makes them understand what's really important.

Nathan glanced over at Sergei, who had a funny smile on his face.

"You're looking pleased with yourself," Nathan said. "Want to let me in on it?"

"I've been doing some thinking," Sergei said. "During all those hours when the *Nina* was in trouble, and I realized I might never see Ludmilla again—I guess it turned my life around."

"Is that why you made that speech about volunteering to stay behind, so that someone else could be saved?"

Sergei grinned, embarrassed. "I guess so. Not much of a hero, am I? I would rather die than feel guilty."

164

"There's nothing wrong with that," Nathan said. "Turned your life around, huh?"

Sergei nodded.

"When Ludmilla and I meet again on Mars, we will have to have a serious talk. I'm going to tell her exactly how I feel. What you said about being too young to make a commitment, and how busy we'll be for the next several years. If she's angry with me, I'll have to live with that. And I'm going to turn over a new leaf now. No more flirting. No more leading one girl on while I make a move on the next one. I'm a new man."

Nathan made a face at him.

"Are you for real? Sergei Chuvakin, the solar system's most famous lady killer, is changing his rep?"

"Absolutely!" Sergei said seriously, then broke into a grin. "For at least the next five minutes!"

"Okay, people, listen up," Dr. Allen said over the intercom. "We've been assigned our flight order. We'll be going in third. The *Nina* first, then the *Pinta,* then us."

Her voice was drowned in protests.

"Hey, no fair!"

" 'Assigned'? Who assigned us?"

"Who's in charge here?"

"We were last in departure order. We should be first on landing!"

"Yeah, we're supposed to be the flagship! What's the deal?"

"It's Dr. Thompson's idea!" Lanie yelled above the others. "Just 'cause he's head of astrophysics and the *Nina*'s his ship—"

165

"Yeah, and Suki Long wins again!" someone else said. "After we saved her butt and the *Nina*'s when they couldn't even get their airlocks open."

"If you're all quite finished . . ." Dr. Allen's voice was crisper than usual. She could hear what was going on. "I'd like to point out that it's really no big deal. As long as we're all down safely, who cares who hits the dirt first?"

"The history books care!" someone shouted. "One small step for a man—"

"—one giant leap for mankind!" Nathan finished. "Everyone remembers Neil Armstrong. Nobody cares much who made the moon landings after him."

"Nobody said anything about who steps out first," Dr. Allen said sharply. That made them think.

"Maybe they'll let one of us," Tara suggested. "That makes perfect sense. If we're the last ship down, we should be the first crew out."

"That makes adults' sense!" Lanie yelled. "Supervisors' sense. It sucks!"

"Calm down, all of you!" Alice said. "Dr. Allen's right. Who cares, as long as we all get there safely? Haven't we been through enough not to care whose footprints are first. They'll all be wiped out by the rest of us walking around, making our imprint. All our names will go in the history books. Earth history books. I don't know about the rest of you, but I've always found history books boring. We're writing our own history down here. Let's not spoil it over something so dumb."

"Roger, *Nina,* we have you in sight," Dr. Allen said into her headset. Beside her in the copilot's seat, Karl felt his hands sweating. He couldn't even wipe them on his pants legs; the fabric of the flight suit was airtight and waterproof. "Monitoring your descent from here on."

"Roger, *Santa Maria.* Estimate we will begin our descent in five minutes—mark. Initiating thruster maneuvers now."

Dr. Allen glanced over at Karl.

"Nervous?"

"Yes"

"Good. If you weren't, I'd worry. Ian, how's the channel through to the *Pinta?*"

"Loud and clear, Doc," he reported from the comm station.

No one on the flying bridge talked after that. All three of them strained their ears to hear Dr. Thompson's voice through the static. Ahead of them they could see the *Nina*'s sleek form beginning the necessary thruster maneuvers.

First it seemed to come to a complete stop above the planet, which simply meant it had slowed its relative speed to coincide with Mars's normal acceleration through space. This would put it, like the robot ships, in geosynchronous orbit above the precise spot where it would touch down. Then, in a series of moves that would make a ballet dancer proud, it began to heel over into a ninety-degree turn.

Where the *Nina* had been running parallel to the surface of Mars, it was now pointed stern end down. The flying-bridge crew wouldn't be able to see where they

167

were going, and would have to rely on the accuracy of their instruments. The forward windshield would be pointed out toward space, and the rearward E.V.A. cameras would have to show the way.

While Karl was thinking about this, the *Nina* had jockeyed into position. Now it began its descent, slowly at first. As it entered Mars's atmosphere, the descent speed would increase. At 21,000 feet, it would be traveling at up to 1,200 miles per hour. It would need to fire its braking thrusters for a full five minutes, then release the nose-cone parachute and coast down. Karl suppressed a shudder. Up until the point where the parachute was released, the crew had only enough control over the descent to abort it if something went wrong. Once the parachute was open, they would have no control at all.

Someone tapped his shoulder from behind. Ian handed him a towel he'd swiped from the gym.

"Me too!" The Irish boy grinned, showing him how his own hands were sweating. "Always prepared!"

"And I'm the one who was in Boy Scouts!" Karl said. He wiped his hands and gave the towel back to Ian. "Thanks — sport."

Ian clapped him on the back. "Bring it down easy, boyo."

"You got it!" Karl said.

". . . getting good radar data . . ." Dr. Thompson's voice filled the headsets inside everyone's helmets, and the intercoms on all three ships. ". . . we have a plus point eighteen yaw, point nine . . . descending

168

smoothly at twelve hundred feet per second . . ."

"Looking good, *Nina*, looking good!" Dr. Allen said, encouraging.

"I wonder if they'll kick up a lot of dust," Sergei said. "Depending on the soil composition and wind direction, it may take a while to settle."

"That's been calculated into the descent procedure," Nathan assured him. "If the *Nina* radios there's too much ground debris, the *Pinta*'s prepared to do one more orbital approach. So are we."

"Well, for our sake, I hope we don't have to," Sergei said. "Two more orbits! I can't stand it!"

"You should have thought of that before you suited up," Nathan said, making Noemi giggle.

Toward the end of its descent, the *Nina* disappeared from the *Santa Maria*'s view. Because of the strong sunlight, the E.V.A. cameras couldn't pick it up this close to the surface. The *Pinta* hove into view over their horizon, standing by to make its descent. Dr. Thompson's last transmission indicated that the parachute had been deployed. Nothing was coming through from the *Nina* now but static. Everyone seemed to have stopped breathing.

"Nine, eight, seven, six, five, four, three," Ian counted off on the digital display. "It should be down. The *Nina* should be down."

"This is Mars ship *Nina* to *Pinta* and *Santa Maria*," Dr. Thompson cut in. His normally calm voice shook with excitement. "We are on the ground. Repeat—"

There was nervous cheering in the corridors.

"One down, two to go," Gen said.

Dr. Thompson reported they had hardly kicked up any dust. The *Pinta* now began its descent. Karl, Ian, and Dr. Allen watched from the flying bridge. Everyone within range of an E.V.A. screen watched as it heeled over in the same way the *Nina* had. Looking good.

In the hydroponics lab, Dr. Berger shut down the rotation mechanism, bringing the great wheel to a standstill. He looked at his plants once more before he put his helmet on.

"Be well, children," he told them. "We're almost there."

He put a final audio tape into the tape deck before he went to lock himself into his restraint harness. As the *Santa Maria*'s thrusters began to fire, the strains of Beethoven's "Ode to Joy" roared triumphantly through the lab and into space.

It was Lisette's idea to link hands throughout the corridors. She saw how scared everyone looked. And if she looked anything like the way she felt inside . . . She tapped the two boys on either side of her.

"Hey," she said, holding out her hands. Each boy grabbed on, and reached out their own hands to those on either side of them. Gen saw what Lisette was doing and started a human chain on his side of the corridor.

They were all sealed off inside their helmets and flight suits, all locked into their restraint harnesses, all cut off from their fellow human beings except through this sense of touch.

As they had when they left Icarus, many people prayed. The whispers carried over the headsets, filling each person's helmet with the sound of many voices.

Karl exhaled as he readjusted his sweating hands on the thruster control. At his touch, the ship stabilized, and began its descent.

Down, down, down they went. The gravity of Mars seemed to reach out and grab them, pulling them down into their boots as they experienced real gravity for the first time in over a year. It was like the first big hill on a roller coaster, going down, down, down with no sense of control. They could feel their eardrums pop. Someone screamed, someone else laughed nervously. They kept going down, down, down.

Were they only getting used to the gravity, or were they actually slowing? The braking thrusters began to fire. They fired for a full five minutes, while everyone stared at the digital display, then stopped. They could neither see nor feel the parachute opening, but Dr. Allen's voice came over the intercom to assure them that it had.

Nathan, who had had his eyes closed all this time, opened them now to read the digital display.

"One minute!" he said so softly no one could hear him. No one had to. They were all thinking the same thing. Fifty-nine seconds until they either soft-landed or . . .

Fifty-five seconds. A lot could happen in fifty-five seconds. Something could overload. Something could malfunction. They could crash, or burn up, or come down on a huge boulder and tip over, crushing half of them before —

"Thirty seconds," Sergei said.

A lot could happen in thirty seconds.

No one breathed. No one could even think. All they could do was count: five, four, three, two . . . Suddenly everything stopped. Time itself seemed to have stopped. The silence seemed to last forever. Then everyone remembered how to breathe again. They began to move around, trying to remember how to move in gravity again.

They were still holding hands. Now they began to squeeze one another's hands, to clap and exchange high-fives and stamp their feet and dance around. No one heard Dr. Allen announcing their arrival on the intercom. No one needed to. A single glorious whoop of joy came from everyone at the same time: "WE'RE HERE!!"

JUMP ABOARD THE MARS ROVER AS NATHAN AND HIS TEAM MUST FIND A LOST SUPPLY SHIP BEFORE THE ENTIRE NEW MARS COLONY IS DESTROYED IN THEIR NEXT EXCITING SPACE ADVENTURE:

THE YOUNG ASTRONAUTS #5:
SPACE PIONEERS

For more information about The Young Astronaut Council, or to start a Young Astronaut Chapter in your school, write to:

THE YOUNG ASTRONAUT COUNCIL
1211 Connecticut Avenue, N.W.
Suite 800
Washington, D.C. 20036